UP CLOSE AND GONE

Also by Jennie Spallone

Up Close and Gone

Smashing Castles

Psychobabble

Fatal Reaction

Window of Guilt

Deadly Choices

Write Me Up!

Up Close and Gone

Jennie Spallone

Up Close and Gone by Jennie Spallone

This book is written to provide information and motivation to readers. Its purpose is not to render any type of psychological, legal, or professional advice of any kind. The content is the sole opinion and expression of the author, and not necessarily that of the publisher.

Copyright © 2021 by Jennie Spallone

All rights reserved. No part of this book may be reproduced, transmitted, or distributed in any form by any means, including, but not limited to, recording, photocopying, or taking screenshots of parts of the book, without prior written permission from the author or the publisher. Brief quotations for noncommercial purposes, such as book reviews, permitted by Fair Use of the U.S. Copyright Law, are allowed without written permissions, as long as such quotations do not cause damage to the book's commercial value.

This is a work of fiction. Any resemblance to the living or dead is entirely coincidental.

ISBN: 978-0-9726768-5-4 (Paperback)
ISBN: 978-0-9726768-6-1 (Digital)

Printed in the United States of America.

To My Loving Husband
who encouraged me
to catapult myself over every hurdle....

Acknowledgements

This book is near and dear to my heart, as it deals with the challenges all mothers and daughters face as they share a life-long balancing act of connection versus independence.

The impact of adoption on a children, siblings, birth parents, and adoptive parents is yet another theme explored in these pages. May positive words fall from our lips to heal the verbal wounds we've inflicted on each other over the years. May we open our heart to listen to, as well as share our own, grievances and resentments toward our family members with the goal of establishing a new beginning filled with positive communications.

In birthing *Up Close and Gone,* I have been fortunate to have Beth Terrell and Sue Toth as my talented midwives, coaching me through copy and developmental editing. Former SINC Murder We Write President Chris Roerden gave me a clean bill of health for my inital pages review, while New York best selling author Lee Child, upon examination of a later draft, told me my book has "merit." Maverick Book Services, helped me deliver my book baby after extensive breathing exercises in book formatting and cover design {assistance from Deposit Photos.com}.

I thank Beta readers Davida Levine, Anna Humphrey, and author Austin Camacho for providing thoughtful feedback on both content and grammar.

Chapter 1

Shana
June 26, 2018
12:35 p.m.

Shana Kahn stormed out of the Boathouse Restaurant, paying little heed to the path she was taking. The relentless sun beat upon her uncovered head like a burning skillet. Sunstroke would be a kinder consequence than reliving the venomous words her daughters had hurled at her over brunch. Humiliated in front of her son-in-law's family whom she'd only just met, Shana planned to hop an Uber from Central Park back to the hotel, then book a flight home to North Carolina.

A hysterical giggle escaped her lips. Rachel and Becca had gifted her and their father David a weekend stay at the hotel where both families were staying. Hell if she could remember its name. A couple of seconds later, a memory marble rolled into consciousness: *U.S. President.*

Determined to Google each president's name until one name resonated, Shana opened her cell phone. *Shit!* The phone was dead, and she'd forgotten to bring the charger. Little chance of locating the correct exit out of the sprawling Park sans GPS or street name to guide her.

Dirty little secret? Shana's sense of direction was zilch, a fact she'd managed to hide from her last four *Chicago Sun-Times* editors before she and dozens of other reporters were forced into retirement.

Thanks to her pre-trip research, Shana did know that Central Park 2.5 miles spanned 843 acres of gardens, meadows, and woods; information overload as she navigated her way through a maze of twists and turns. Finally, she hit a landmark: Belvedere Castle. Fanning her sweat-soaked silk shirt, Shana checked out a map board; its interconnected symbols and curvy lines made her eyes glaze over.

Exhausted and thirsty, Shana headed to a nearby water fountain and gulped its tepid water like Cheerwine soda. As she stepped away from the fountain, a young mother took her place. Shana gazed into the buggy. "Your baby is so adorable!" Her first white lie of the day.

The young mother's eyes glowed with pleasure. "Thank you!"

"Listen, I got separated from my family. Could I borrow your phone to call my kids?"

Shana couldn't fault the young woman's wary expression as she took in her purple streaked hair and disheveled appearance; hell, she would have reacted in similar fashion had their situation been reversed. The young woman hesitantly pulled a leopard-covered iPhone from her Prada. "Here you go."

Shana let out the deep breath she'd been holding and punched in Rachel's number.

"Hello?" a voice asked breathlessly.

At the sound of her pregnant daughter's anxious voice, Shana knew she was in for a lifetime of recriminations. She abruptly clicked off the phone. "No answer. Thanks, anyway."

The young mother grabbed her cell phone from Shana and briskly stepped on the buggy release. "I hope you find your family soon."

Shana watched the mother and child disappear into the throng of joggers and bikers. Phone dead. No charger. Rachel and Becca would chalk up her *lost in the park* anecdote to just one more example of her impulsivity.

Suck it up, she told herself. Just one more humiliation through which she'd be forced to crawl.

Chapter 2

BECCA

From across the restaurant courtyard, Becca glimpsed her sister and brother-in-law chatting animatedly with his family. This was the first time Zander had reconnected with his family in ten years. It was also the first time her family had met his stepdad Aamer, twelve years older than Zan. Infuriated that his mother had chosen a soulmate so close in age, he'd taken revenge by not inviting the family to his wedding. Today was a fresh start for both their families. Becca hoped her mom didn't fuck it up, which was why she was standing guard as Mom rose on tippy toes to give Aamer a bear hug.

"It is absolutely wonderful to finally meet you!"

Becca rolled her eyes. For a former news reporter, her mom sure used a lot of meaningless adjectives. The top of her head reached only to the chest of the burly man, so she couldn't pretend to smash into his dark sunglasses. With Mom, you never knew if she was pranking you or just being a klutz.

"You as well, Shana," said the John Belushi lookalike.

Mom released him, then opened her fire engine-red lips to speak. "Your wife mentioned you drive an Uber. That must save your family a lot of money in cab fare!"

"Mom!"

Becca's mother glared at her.

Aamer chuckled. "Your mama tells true."

Shana raised her chin at Becca, as if to say *I told you so*. Then she asked Aamer a couple of non-confrontational questions about growing up in the Middle East; the foods his mother prepared, special festivals they celebrated, family life—a similar routine designed to inspire trust in the people she interviewed so they'd blab their sad truths for her newspaper readers.

Oblivious to her Mom's intent, Aamer was in the zone. He leaned against a white brick wall of the restaurant, his ankles crossed. He removed his black hat and wiped sweaty dribbles. Then he relayed an anecdote about his peaceful childhood in Iran, pre-ISIS.

Shana glanced across the courtyard, where the two families were laughing it up. Becca could almost see the gears in her mother's brain give her a thumbs-up to operate freely until their brunch buzzer sounded. Shana planted her feet in a semi-wide stance. Uh oh! Becca knew that stance. She sneezed, attempting to distract her mother.

Her mother ignored her.

"May I ask you a difficult question?" Mom's sugary voice was enough to cause a diabetic coma. "One that may upset you?"

"Shana, no subject be out bound."

The poor guy was clueless to her Mom's intent.

"Are you sure? Because Rachel made me promise to keep our conversation light."

Her mother's concern could charm the fins off a rainbow trout.

"No thing you ask will hurt feelings, Shana."

Shana opened her mouth. "Does the Koran…"

Becca leaned forward to pinch her upper arm, but her mom stepped sideways, and she fell. She'd been an idiot for wearing three-inch heels through Central Park, but this was her first time visiting New York City.

Aamer lifted her to her feet. He pulled a handkerchief from his pocket and pressed the clean cloth to her skinned knees. "It only bleed a little bit."

Eager to finish asking her question, Becca's mother was oblivious to her mishap.

"…believe in peace or in violence?"

The remainder of her mother's question echoed through Becca's ears.

"We'll be right back!"

Becca grabbed Shana's arm and limped into the adjacent garden. "You promised Rachel not to ask Zander's family any personal questions!"

Her mother yanked her arm from Becca's clutches and headed back to Aamer. "Becca is worried that I have embarrassed her pregnant sister by asking you these questions."

Aamer's eyes grew wide. "Praised be Allah!"

Becca paled. Rachel and Zander hadn't told him they were having a baby. Her mom would be dead meat when Rachel got hold of her.

Unaware the moon had changed course, Aamer responded to Shana's question. "Koran speaks of love and peace."

"Then why does ISIS claim the Koran as its bible?" Shana persisted.

Aamer's smile dipped one iota. "Christians kill thousands of non-beliefs in name of God, no?"

Her mother had gone too far. Everybody knew religion and politics were off limits.

Becca nudged her mother with her hip. This time their body parts connected.

Shana winced. "Touché!"

Becca wasn't sure if her comment was meant for her or for Aamer. Rules meant nothing to her mother. Sometimes this worked in her favor. She'd walk up to a homeless person, hand him a cheese sandwich, and ask how he wound up on the street. People rose to the occasion once they trusted she was interested in their responses. It made Becca proud she was her mom.

Today was not one of those days.

Aamer's expression was impenetrable behind his dark sunglasses. "In fact, I enjoy this subject very much."

"I'd love to learn more about your culture," said Shana.

Becca groaned.

"Please feel free to ask."

Fortunately, their table for twelve was called. Becca, Shana, and Aamer caught up with their respective families and made their way into the boat house. Was it by accident that Aamer chose a seat at the opposite end of the brunch table, she wondered?

Becca slipped into the seat next to her dad. Her cheeks felt like volcanic ash, but unlike her mother, she knew how to keep her mouth shut. A quick glance around the table confirmed that Zander's extended family members were oblivious to Shana's interrogation.

Her lips pressed tight, Becca's mom took a seat next to her and her dad. Shana gazed out the picture window. Becca could tell she was pissed off at not getting to ask her full repertoire of questions. How many times did she and Rachel need to remind their mom that she was a retired reporter—*retired* being the key word. No one enjoyed answering her intrusive questions.

Rachel and Zander smiled broadly as they took their seats across from them. Confident she'd received a Get out of Jail Free Card, Mom's expression brightened. She reached out for a group hug.

Platters of eggs, pork sausages, steamed spinach, banana bread, and fruit adorned the linen clothed table, erasing the awkward encounter from everyone's mind. Through the window, they stared at families rowing on the lake, sun shining, skies bright blue, leafy trees reflected in the water. Peaceful. Like a Monet painting.

When their waiter stopped to refill their crystal water glasses, Shana glanced up at him. "Could you please turn down the air-conditioning? It's freezing in here."

The young waiter adjusted the bow tie of his tuxedo. "But of course."

Rachel rolled her eyes. "You should have brought your sweater."

"So kill me now!"

Becca's sister removed her shorty sweater and handed it across the table. "Don't ask the waiter to do anything else for you!"

Breastfed on drama, it was no wonder Becca taught acting.

Becca's dad calmly chewed his as he observed yet one more Kahn family drama. Shana hotly turned to him. "Aren't you going to say something?"

Becca's dad shook his head. "This is between you and the girls."

"You never think before you open your mouth!" Rachel blurted in a snarky stage whisper. "All you do is embarrass us."

Her mom's eyes grew big, like she'd been slapped in the face. She stood and pushed her wooden chair back from the table. "Sorry I'm not perfect. Maybe you're better off without me!"

Becca wanted to say something to ease the tension, but her words would be dishonest. Mom's hands trembled as she tossed the shorty sweater back to Rachel. "I'll meet you on the patio."

"But you haven't eaten since early this morning," Becca protested.

Her mom raised her chin in a haughty pose. Then she made her way down the table. Becca got up to follow, but her dad touched her wrist. "She just needs a breath of fresh air. She'll be fine."

For a moment, Becca wavered. Her mom was so sensitive. She'd lived away from home for nine years, but her dad lived with her 24/7. He knew what she needed.

Becca was about to sit again when her mom called her name.

"I forgot my purse." Shana's voice was as cold as lemon ice. "It's hanging on my chair."

Becca sidled past the seated family members and did a quick search for her mother's purse. As usual, it wasn't where it's supposed to be. Then she remembered. "You left your purse in the hotel room."

With a huff, Mom turned and headed toward the front of the restaurant. As Becca watched her go, she pretended they were actors who would return to their hotel that night without harboring hurt feelings toward one other.

Then she noticed Aamer's chair was empty.

CHAPTER 3

SHANA

Shana continued along the forested trail. She needed to get to the nearest boutique or eatery. Once there, she'd call her daughters from the cashier's phone, tell them she got mugged at the Park—her second white lie of the day—and ask them to pick her up. Rachel and Becca would act loving and concerned, their earlier fury forgotten. Oops! They knew she didn't have her purse on her. Perhaps an assault in the woods would sound more convincing. She felt her heart begin to beat overtime. Too scary to even lie about.

The big question was whether she could convince her husband and kids to believe any story she told them. Her family knew she was capable of saying anything—doing anything—to wiggle off the hook. After twenty-six years as a reporter for *The Chicago Sun-Times*, Shana could talk her way out of almost any predicament. David bragged about the time she convinced a pimp to release his sex workers so she could write a complimentary profile on him. It would have been a terrific story, too, if the CPD hadn't whisked the low-life out from under her, figuratively speaking.

What if her daughters didn't want her back in their lives, with her bossy, busybody behavior? The very idea threw Shana into a thought spasm. She practiced her deep breathing to calm down. Of course her kids loved her, she told herself. They'd do anything for her. Without a doubt, her husband would come for her—if he wasn't enveloped in a photography project.

As Shana noted the busy traffic off in the distance, tentacles of anxiety wrapped themselves around her gut. Sunday traffic in Chicago was moderate, sports lovers taking to the expressways. North Carolina's small-town traffic was minimal on a Sunday, folks returning from church to hang out with family. But Sunday traffic in New York City was serious shit.

Then she recalled the horse-driven carriage rides brochure. Nothing wrong with asking for help; how many times had she chastised David for not doing so when driving through an unfamiliar area? Following her own advice, she asked a jogger to confirm the carriage stand's location.

Once at the carriage stand, Shana negotiated with a young turbaned driver for a free carriage ride to the exit, then immediately canceled, still clueless as to her family's original starting point. Shivering in the heat of her predicament, Shana caught sight of a playground and duck pond. She began walking toward the welcome distraction when she noticed the darkening skies. Rain soon pounded families and joggers as they fled the park. But Shana didn't care about getting drenched. The rain was a welcome release. She flung her arms to the heavens and twirled in place.

Then, a tall, well-dressed young man stepped into Shana's path. Wordlessly, he extended a golf umbrella toward her. People were so wrong when they said New Yorkers didn't give a damn, she thought as she gratefully moved underneath the clothed shelter.

"Thank you so much! I always tell my kids a stranger is just a friend you haven't yet met!"

The young man grinned, his eyes twinkling. At the same moment, Shana felt a sharp prick above her left hip.

As she started to black out, she heard him say, "Enjoy this moment. The worst is yet to come."

Chapter 4

BECCA

Zander's mom Oma noticed Becca's stare. "Aamer delivers flowers on weekends. He must have gotten called away. Your mother also left the table. She looked pale. Is she feeling okay?"

Wouldn't it make more sense to drive your Uber on the weekends, when you could make the most money?" wondered Becca. Either way, it was none of her business. She refused to be a busybody like the woman who birthed her. But, like her mother, she was not above telling a white lie.

"Mom's got indigestion."

She and Rachel felt bad for their daddy. Mom loved him; they've been married four decades. But their personalities were as different as Sonny and Cher, at least from what Becca had seen on T.V. reruns. A lifetime of bickering and making up. It made her doubt she'd ever get married.

Becca's dad dabbed his lips with a linen napkin. Hat slanted over one eye, he could model for *GQ Magazine, 65 Plus Edition*—except there was no such edition. He had a knee problem and walked with a cane. Last night, it had taken them two hours instead of the GPS's twenty-minutes to trek from the hotel to Times Square. Rachel, Zander's younger brother Kaiden, and Becca had taken turns walking at her dad's side. But Shana had been impatient. She'd walk ahead for a city block, then turn and holler, "Come on, David!"

It wasn't like her mom tried to be difficult, but her high-powered persona was stuck on the conveyor belt, refusing to surrender to retirement. It had only been a couple of months since she'd been put out to pasture. Becca tried to convince herself that her mother would eventually shave those sharp edges. Like Alexander Pope once wrote, *hope springs eternal.*

Despite her dad's protests, Zan and Kaiden insisted on splitting their brunch bill. Zan's two-year-old nephew was cranky and crying for his nap. Oma hugged Becca and her dad and headed back to the hotel with the rest of her family.

Becca made a beeline for the bathroom to check on her mom. She wasn't in there.

Outside, dozens of people milled around the brick patio, waiting for their buzzers to zzzzz. No sign of Shana. She went back inside the restaurant.

Sports programs blared from three televisions mounted above the lobby bar. Nada.

Becca approached the lady behind the cash register. The woman gave her a harried expression, as if she had a line of people waiting for her to process their credit cards, instead of just her. "Yes?"

"Did you see an older woman with purple-streaked blond hair walk out the door?"

"Hundreds of people come through here day and night."

"Do they all have purple hair?" Becca tossed the hasty retort over her shoulder.

Once again, she stepped outside and into the sunlight. She wondered if her mom was pissed off enough to hail an Uber back to their hotel. She was about to punch her number into her cell phone when she remembered that Shana's battery had died en route to Central Park. How many times did she and Rachel have to remind her to charge her phone every night like the rest of the universe did? Why cause them needless worry about her whereabouts?

Becca was beginning to freak out. Where the hell was her mother? A slight queasiness threatened. Frantic, she searched for an inconspicuous spot to throw up, when she felt a tap on her shoulder. She whirled around to find her dad staring at her.

"I thought you and your mom got locked in the bathroom! Everything okay?"

A loaded question on so many levels. "Upset stomach."

"Mom talking to a stranger in there?"

"She's not in the bathroom." Becca steeled herself for his next question.

"Odds are she's walking around the lake or chatting up the vendors."

"You're probably right."

"I'll get the rest of the crew and we'll head out."

"Good idea." Becca's stomach was cramping like hell, but she managed to keep her body upright.

Her dad squinted at her. "Maybe you should lay off the sausage."

No reason to mention she'd crossed out processed meat from her diet. Her sister was a health nut; she'd nagged her until she'd surrendered.

"What you need is an ice-cold ginger ale."

Becca smiled wanly. "Thanks."

Her dad disappeared back into the restaurant. Grasping her aching tummy, she abandoned the premises and headed down a path leading to the vendors. What kind of mother deserts her kids on a family outing? Her heart whispered: a mother who feels her kids don't give a damn about her.

Soon Becca came to a row of horse-driven carriages, their drivers hawking their services. "A dollar a minute!" Her GPS indicated the main exit was eight miles away. Maybe her mom rode a carriage to an exit; judging by the sprawling landscape, there must be several of them. Which path would she take?

Fur Elyse echoes from her phone. Becca clicked. "Hey, Rach."

"Where are you guys? Dad's got your ginger ale, and we're all standing outside on the patio like idiots."

Once again, barf threatened to bomb her esophagus. "It's a long story."

"Just tell me where to meet you. Ouch. Just felt the baby kick!"

No way could Becca tell her their mom was missing. If she lost the baby, it would be her fault!

"Meet us by the carriage rides." Becca clicked off.

Striving to swallow her panic, Becca stumbled over to the drivers. "Excuse me, did any of you drive a middle-aged woman with purple-streaked blond hair, maybe like ten minutes ago?"

The men shook their turbaned heads.

Then a young, brown-skinned driver turned to a bearded driver. "What mean purple-streaked?"

The bearded driver replied in a foreign language.

The young driver's face brightened. "I see this lady. She say she forget purse at hotel. I offer lady free ride to exit. She say 'no thank you,' then leave."

"Thanks for trying to help her."

"She is related to you?" the young driver asked.

Becca's anguish broke free. "She's my mother!"

Before the driver could apologize, she turned and stumbled down the road.

She visualized finding her mom; Shana would fall into her arms and she'd comfort her. Shana was 4 ½ inches shorter than her, so she couldn't even fall into her mother's arms. How fucked up was that?

Becca shielded her eyes and looked ahead. The skies were beginning to darken and a spatter of raindrops fell on her head and arms. No sign of her mom. The stomach cramps hurt worse than when she got her period. She fell to her knees. A couple of guys jogged past her without a second glance. Becca punched the hotel number into her phone. The operator confirmed that no one fitting her mom's description had entered the lobby, gift shop, or bar area within the last hour.

Fur Elyse again. Becca hit *ignore* and punched in *911*.

"What is your emergency?"

The words blew through her lips like a hurricane. "My mother is missing."

"How long has she been gone?"

She checked her cell phone. "Forty-seven minutes."

"Are you in danger?"

"No."

"Where are you calling from?"

"Central Park."

"Let me guess. You're visiting New York and you and your mother got separated in the park."

The blacktop was burning her knees. Unsteadily, she rose to her feet.

"I need to find my mother, make sure she's okay!"

"She's been gone less than an hour. Have you tried her cell phone?"

Rachel's number appeared on her phone screen. She wouldn't give up! Again, she hit *ignore*.

"My mom's cell died earlier today," Becca yelled into the phone.

"Trust me, she'll take an Uber back to your hotel and phone you from there."

An opaque screen slid through Becca's brain, making her dizzy.

"My mom left her purse in the hotel room. She's got no money to pay for a ride. We're miles from the hotel."

It was raining bullets, now. Soaked, she limped toward an ice cream stand for shelter.

"Happens all the time, hon. Moms are resourceful. I guarantee you'll find each other soon. If not, call us back."

"She could be kidnapped or dead. I need to find her now!"

"Is your mother mentally challenged?"

Becca wiped the rain from her eyes. "Stubborn but not crazy."

"A danger to herself or others?"

As a reporter, she once put an attacker in a choke hold and kicked him in the balls, her prowess adopted after a mere two self-defense classes. "No."

"So you're telling me you're not in danger, your mother is not mentally challenged, and she is not a danger to herself or others, that right?"

"Yes, but...."

"She could have made an unscheduled shopping trip."

"I told you, she doesn't have her purse on her!"

"Look, I need to go. Good luck finding your mom. She'll be fine, you'll see."

Becca was about to argue when the phone went dead.

Fur Elyse floated through the air. "Hello?"

Rachel's voice was thick with tears. "We're at the carriage stall, getting drenched. Where the hell are you and Mom?"

Pictures of their mom, blindfolded and whisked into a bad guy's van, streamed through Becca's brain. Her heart was straining like a Rottweiler on a leash. For Rach's sake, she attempted to slow her breathing.

"There's been a change of plans.

"Change of plans? We're supposed to see the sites today. Let me talk to Mom."

Becca squeezed her eyes shut, then blurted. "Mom *is* the change of plans."

"What the hell are you talking about? Put Mom on the phone, now!"

"No can do."

"Why not?" she yelled into the phone.

"Because Mom is not with me!"

"What are you saying? Where is she?"

Becca breathed in and out deeply. "She's gone!"

"What do you mean gone? You said she's with you."

"I lied," she sobbed into the phone.

Rachel must have been on speaker phone because their dad's voice came on the line. "It's all right, Becca." His voice was calm, with only a hint of unease. "Slow down and tell me what happened."

Becca relived the whole story for him.

In the background, she heard Zander comforting Rachel. She wanted to die.

"If your mother hoofed it back to the hotel, that would take a while, wouldn't it?" asked her dad.

She grimaced. *Denial* was their dad's middle name.

Rachel came back on the phone. "Why would she leave us in the first place?"

Luckily, her sister was unaware of the ISIS conversation between Mom and Aamer. Becca fell on her sword. "It's my fault. I should have followed her when she left the table."

Dad came back on the phone. "Girls, stop beating yourselves up. Mom's back at the hotel. You'll see."

Becca prayed dad was right.

Then she gasped, remembering.

Aamer was gone, too.

Coincidence? Or maybe he wasn't off delivering flowers, after all.

Chapter 5

Alan
January 8, 1983

Overcome with emotion, Alan held his eight-day-old infant for only the third time since Justin's birth. The new father ran his index finger along his son's tiny chin. He kissed each doll-sized toe. God had answered by granting them not one but three babies, yet only Justin had been born alive; his organs shutting down even as Alan kissed those precious toes. How could a father and mother allow their sweet infant to undergo needless suffering when certain death loomed near? Alan implored God to cradle the baby's soul. Tears streaming down his cheeks, Alan removed the breathing tube from his son's nostrils.

A collective wave of grief spread through the hospital room as the respiration monitor receded into a flat-line. Instead of joining his wife's family in that emotional swampland, Alan recited the *Shehecheyanu*:

> *Blessed are you Lord our God, Ruler of the Universe who has given us life, sustained us, and allowed us to reach this joyous Day!*

The sobbing in the room ceased. Horrified, everyone turned to Alan. In the silence, he heard their accusation: How can you celebrate your newborn son's death?

After sighing a sigh deeper than the Dead Sea, Alan opened his lips to explain, but the words refused to disentangle themselves from his soul. He was a father forced too soon to release his child unto the spiritual world. The same father who'd experienced a shameful whiff of relief after unhooking his son's breathing apparatus.

"Why?" whispered Amy, his niece, who'd recently celebrated her Bat Mitzvah.

For her sake alone, Alan willed himself to unlock the cavern of his heart.

"I praise God because He decreed my wife shall live, even though he chose to recall our triplets to heaven."

"Only God should make that final judgment," lamented his mother-in-law Libby.

His sister-in-law's accusing eyes drilled into him. "Justin could have lived."

Riddled with grief, Alan willed his words forward. "I give thanks that God enabled me to fulfill the commandment to circumcise my son on the eighth day, as is written. 'I shall make a covenant between me and the children of Israel.'"

Jacob, Amy's younger brother, asked: "If God kept Justin alive to reach this day, why did you take his breathing tube away?"

Each word hit Alan's ears like cement bricks. Had his decision really been that of compassion, he worried, or had that momentary relief revealed his evil inclination?

Just then, Rabbi Shapiro entered the hospital room. He took one look at the faces of those assembled, then walked toward the bassinet and peeked inside. His breath caught. He closed his eyes and began to pray in Hebrew. Even though Alan and Deborah had been raised as Conservative Jews, neither of them understood more than rudimentary Hebrew. But at this moment, Rabbi Shapiro's blessed utterances spread comfort to him and his wife's family.

Alan waited a respectful amount of time for Rabbi Shapiro to conclude his prayers. Then he haltingly spoke.

"Justin had a hole in his heart, his kidney function was failing, and his lungs were shutting down. His prognosis was hours, not days, not months. Deborah and I chose to spare him a horrible death by returning him to his Maker and his two brothers in heaven."

Jerry, Alan's brother, started to interrupt, but Rabbi Shapiro shushed him.

"This is a family decision. We are not to judge. May God watch over Justin's soul, and the souls of all those on earth and in heaven. Amen."

Amen echoed throughout the room.

Alan shook hands with Rabbi Shapiro and exited the hospital room.

A hospital room of individuals who, but for Rabbi Shapiro, was filled with bitterness.

Chapter 6

Becca
June 26, 2018
6:00 P.M.

Dad, Rachel, Zander, and Becca burst into the nearest police station to file a missing person's report. A Detective Stella Hernandez of the 17th precinct was assigned to the case. Forty-something, she guessed. The detective looked kind of crusty. Weathered. Like she'd seen stuff.

"Is there any reason your mother would abruptly leave a family brunch?" she asked.

Rachel massaged her tummy. "Mom was angry with Becca and me."

Zander flung his arm around her shoulders. "Your mother wouldn't allow an argument to come between you guys. She loves you."

"Maybe Mom booked a flight back to North Carolina," Becca said.

"She wouldn't do that, Becca," Dad said.

Rachel began to cry. "It's obvious that none of us really know what she'd do! I say she's been kidnapped. I received a phone call from a strange number today around three p.m. When I answered, the caller hung up."

Becca's stomach churned. "Same thing happened to me about an hour later. I called back. A young woman answered. She asked me to stop prank-calling her and hung up. Maybe Mom borrowed her phone to call us."

Detective Hernandez turned her attention to Dad. "Does your wife know anyone in the city besides your son-in-law's family?"

Dad shook his head. "It's her first time visiting here. Ours, too."

"Has your mother ever impromptu left your family before?"

Dad answered for the family. "My wife marches to her own drummer, but this tune she's not played."

The detective glanced at dad appreciatively. "You have a good command of the English language."

"He and my mom both worked at the same newspaper," Rachel said impatiently. "So what's your plan, Detective?"

Now the detective was all business. "I've got all your information written down. If your mother hasn't come home by 1 p.m. tomorrow, call us back and we'll go from there."

"What the hell!" said Rachel. "You're making us wait 24 hours before you send a search party out for her?"

"Hey, I'm doing you folks a favor and skirting protocol because you're from out-of-state. We don't take a report until a person's gone 24 hours."

David raised his palms upward. "We all appreciate you taking the time to help us, Detective. As you can imagine, we are quite distraught over my wife's disappearance. What is our next step?"

"And what's your plan if our mother is still gone tomorrow?" asked Rachel.

"Let's hope she returns before then. Should that not be the case, we will interview park vendors and restaurant staff."

"Are you going to send out a search and rescue team?" Becca asked. "Mom could have twisted her ankle or had an allergic reaction to poison ivy."

"To be honest, anything could have happened. We've got lakes, wooded trails, all kinds of plants, insects."

"OMG." Becca's voice shook. "She could have fallen in the lake."

Rachel rolled her eyes. "Reeling in a shark?"

"Sharks swim in oceans, not in man-made lakes."

"Exactly!"

"Besides, Mom doesn't swim or fish, does she?" Becca asked.

Rachel raised her eyebrows.

"Hey, I've lived away from home for nine years. Maybe she's taken up a couple new hobbies you guys forgot to mention."

"Yeah, right."

"Knock it off, girls," said Dad. "Right now, we've got more important fish to fry."

Rachel laughed so hard, tears streamed down her cheeks. "Get it? 'Fish to fry.'"

Detective Hernandez discreetly shuffled her notes.

"If our mother is being held captive, how are you going to find the perpetrator?" Rachel's question was the elephant in the room.

Becca's sister knew detective terminology upside down and right side up. She'd watched every detective show imaginable, from *Law & Order SVU* to *Blacklist*.

"We have special park police, as well as the NYPD," said the detective. "We'll put out a missing person's alert on cell phone and cable television."

"We can post Mom's picture on Facebook," Becca said.

"Good idea. I suggest you all go back to your hotel in case she returns."

Rachel massaged her belly. "In case? You mean 'when.'"

Detective Hernandez dialed her office phone. "We're hoping for the best outcome."

Rachel got up to use the bathroom. Clear liquid streamed down her legs and onto the floor.

"OMG!" said Becca. "I've Googled pregnancy; that stream is not pee."

Rachel gazed at the wet floor. Her face paled. "My water broke!"

"But you're only twenty-six weeks!" Becca blurted.

Minutes later, paramedics lifted her sister onto a gurney and wheeled her out of the building and into an ambulance. Zander climbed inside while Dad and Becca slipped into his car to follow them to New York Presbyterian Hospital.

Dad keyed the ignition and pulled their rental car away from the curb. A yellow ticket peeked from behind the windshield wipers. Becca could tell he was upset because instead of stopping the car to retrieve the police ticket, Dad pressed the wiper button and the ticket flew away. "Your sister will be fine," he said, his tone robotic.

"It's too soon for the baby to be born. She's only the size of a zucchini!"

"Your sister and the baby are in God's hands. They'll be fine."

For all of their sakes, Becca hoped he was right.

Chapter 7

RACHEL

Rachel's obstetrician removed the stethoscope from around her neck and stood over the hospital bed. "The good news is there is no infection."

"And the bad news?" asked Rachel.

"You'll need to stay on bedrest here at the hospital until you deliver."

"But she's over three months early," Zan protested.

"Which is why your baby's lungs need to further develop."

"I need my mom."

Doctor Nayman looked concerned. "Have you contacted her?"

"Her mother is missing," Zan interrupted.

The doctor blanched. "I'm so sorry."

"Which is why my wife's water broke, right?"

The doctor gave them an empathetic smile. "It is true that catastrophic stress can cause the placenta to produce a hormone called CRH, which can trigger the release of prostaglandins and uterine contractions. However, your wife was not experiencing close contractions when she arrived at the hospital. We are administering anti-contraction medicine so she does not go into premature labor."

"So I'm just supposed to lie here until my baby is born?" Rachel sniffled, swiping her nose with a tissue. Being confined to bedrest because of her mother's actions—for she still believed it to be so, despite her doctor's non-confirmation—was yet one more example of her disregard for anybody but herself. How many times had their family attended her soccer matches without mom because she was hot on the trail of tracking down a witness in a criminal case? How many times had Rachel teased her about studying to become a private investigator; she'd be away from the family for the same number of hours but make more money. I'm too busy to be with you guys, let alone go back to school at my age, she'd say.

The doctor smiled. "In a few days, you will be moved to an antepartum room, which has a refrigerator and a sitting area. You will have your blood drawn every three days, so the blood bank has blood on hand for you in the event you need a transfusion. We will be on the lookout for infection. You will have your vitals taken every eight hours, and fetal monitoring at least twice a day."

"Great," muttered Rachel.

"What are the visiting hours? Her father and sister will want to visit."

"We are very liberal here, as long as it is not past ten p.m."

Rachel began to sob. "The only visitor I need to walk through that door is my mother!"

Zan took her hands in his. "The detective is working on that, Honey."

"Then why isn't Mom here?" Rachel lamented.

The doctor's eyes shone with empathy. "We will speak again. Know that both you and your baby are in good hands."

Rachel reached out to touch her arm. "Sorry I was being a brat. We appreciate you."

The doctor nodded and left.

"What if my words hurt Mom so bad, she never comes back? What if she's been killed?"

Zan tenderly swept strands of tear-stained hair from her face. "Right now, our baby's life depends on you staying calm."

"Ouch!" Rachel rubbed her tummy.

Zan reached for the nurse buzzer, but she stopped him. "I'm okay."

"You sure?"

Rachel nodded.

"How about trying that deep breathing stuff you do?"

"Fine, but pray for me and the baby."

Zan grimaced. "You know God and I don't mesh."

Rachel smiled as she closed her eyes. "Do it for me."

DAY 1

POST-KIDNAPPING

CHAPTER 8

SHANA

Shana regained consciousness to discover her arms shackled to a lead-speckled radiator against the wall opposite a kitchen sink. Sunlight dripped through a filthy window above the sink.

Rat-a-tat steps bounded into the kitchen. Before her stood the nice young man who'd shared his umbrella. "How'd you sleep?'

"Where am I?" Shana asked, bewildered.

'You passed out in Central Park and I brought you back to my grandparents' house so I could attend to you," he said, smiling.

"Why didn't you bring me to the nearest hospital? And why are my arms shackled?"

"You had no money, health insurance card, or identification on you. I was afraid the hospital would consider you indigent and turn you away. The shackles were just meant to keep you safe. You tried to hurt yourself."

Twenty-six years as a newspaper reporter enabled Shana's bullshit detector to flush out many a loser. This guy was no exception. "Thanks for your help, but my arms are numb. Please unlock these shackles."

The young man knelt by Shana's side and gazed into her brown-green eyes. "You were acting crazy last night, scratching at your wrists, shrieking for no apparent reason. I prefer to release your shackles once a family member comes to fetch you. Then I'll know you're safe."

"If that's your plan, I first need to use the bathroom. Then I need to let my kids know I'm all right and text them your address. To do that, I need you to unlock this contraption."

Shana watched the young man produce a flip phone from his pocket. What an odd phone choice for a millennial. It had been at least twenty years since she, herself, had carried one of those antiquated cell phones, preceded by pocket pagers. Pocket pagers had proved a boom for the newspaper industry. When she and her fellow reporters would receive a beep—she'd set hers to 1 beep for office (a lead), 2 beeps for personal calls (a need)—they'd rush to the nearest phone booth to return the call. Freaking frustrating was when those mad dashes to a telephone booth resulted in a telephone solicitation.

"Do you want me to repeat it?"

Her eyebrows scrunched. "Repeat what?"

"I was just saying I understand your predicament. Please allow me to punch in the numbers for you."

His was a disposable phone. She'd bet her favorite hair dye on it. Thank goodness for Amazon. Flipping through the online shades of purple, she'd ultimately settled on grape over peacock blue; paying that price tag would have been indulgent, now that she was retired.

"Hello?"

No way could she expose her family to this psycho by giving him their phone number.

"That's okay. Just release these shackles, and I'll phone the kids myself."

"No worries. I can manage."

Even if she did, he'd use the prefix *67 so his call couldn't be traced. "Let me think about it."

The young man's posture stiffened. "I saved your life, but you don't trust me to phone your kids?"

Shana reconsidered giving him their number. Her family would hear his voice, perhaps even record it if they were sharp enough. "I apologize. If you meant me harm, you would have already acted upon it."

The young man yanked her shackles down to the base of the radiator. "Bitch!"

His abrupt tone was a bad omen. Shana's stomach roiled as she struggled to come up with an anger-diffuser. Perhaps agreeing with him was the key.

"My kids would second your label of me."

The young man spat in her face.

Anger welled up inside her. "Wipe my face immediately!"

He hit her leg with his fist. "Lady, you have no clue who you're dealing with, what I'm capable of doing. You want to get out of here, give me your family's phone number. Now!"

"Why am I here? If it's ransom you want, my husband's got plenty of money to pay for my release." Her third white lie in less than twenty-four hours.

Her captor's laugh sounded like something from a *Halloween 5* remake. "I never mentioned ransom, and you are not in charge!" he said, punching her in the arm. "Give me the number!"

Shana stiffened. "No way."

He assumed a Downward Dog pose. She giggled hysterically. Another yoga enthusiast!

His face reddened. "Do as I say, Whore!"

Shana willed herself to stay calm. She'd been made scared shitless by the best of them, from Mafia kingpins to corrupt CEOs. This loser was no contender. "That all you got?" she taunted.

He came at her, fists raised.

Time to do the unexpected. Shana slid down from her knees to her haunches. Then she scrunched her eyelids. "Go ahead. Kill me. I've embarrassed my family numerous times. They won't search for me."

In one quick move, he dug a pen knife from his pocket and slashed her right cheek.

Shana's eyes flew open. At the sight of her own blood creeping from her cheek down her right arm, she let loose a pool of pee.

Her captor jumped to his feet. "Ugh!" He shoved a roll of paper towels toward her. "Clean it up!" Each word a rifle bullet.

Shana leaned her cheek toward her shackled arms and sniffed. "Ugh! My blood smells worse than my piss!"

He pulled her hair up so her eyes met his. "Do you really want Rachel and Becca to discover their mother's been hacked into soup chunks?"

Shana's eyes widened in horror.

He knew her daughters' names.

Not random.

The room seemed to spin.

The last thing she saw before slipping into darkness was the slight smile on the young man's face.

CHAPTER 9

ALAN
JANUARY 9, 1983
FUNERAL

After Justin and his stillborn brothers were buried—each in his own tiny casket—Alan and Deborah headed back to their one-story house to prepare for mourners who would soon pile through their front door. Sitting Shiva was not required if a baby lived less than thirty days, but his wife had insisted on observing the ritual.

"Two days ago, we were looking forward to bringing three babies home. Today we return home empty-handed. God owes us this much."

As soon as Alan unlocked the door to their house, Deborah swept past him. Gut wrenching sounds echoed from the master bathroom. A random thought struck him; he could wait until after shiva to clean the toilet, since the mourners would use the hall bathroom.

The mourners began to arrive. A plastic smile on his lips, Alan accepted perfunctory hugs, as well as multiple dishes of fruit, kosher sweets, and dairy platters. When Deborah returned to the living room, a touch of lipstick emphasizing her paleness, Rabbi Shapiro began to lead the mourners in prayer. Although it wasn't the traditional Kaddish prayer, due to the brief amount of time the babies had lived, the chanting of the Hebrew words soothed him.

When Rabbi Shapiro finished, Alan went into the kitchen to prepare a plate of food for his wife; all she'd consumed today was a cup of chicken broth and a couple of bites of challah.

Rabbi Shapiro joined him at the kitchen island. "How are you holding up?"

"Deborah's the one you should be asking."

"You must recognize your own loss," Rabbi Shapiro counseled. "Your pain is no less real than your wife's."

"A man is supposed to protect his family. I let my children slip like marbles through my fingers. I deserve nothing."

Rabbi Shapiro placed his arm around Alan's stooped figure. "Their deaths had nothing to do with you. God works in mysterious ways."

Alan's jaw dropped. "Really? That's all you've got?"

"How many miscarriages did you and Deborah undergo before becoming pregnant with the triplets? How many fertility treatments?"

Alan stared at Rabbi Shapiro. "What's your point?"

"When all hope seemed lost, what happened? God enabled her to become pregnant."

"One more mistake," Alan muttered.

"God does not make mistakes."

Alan opened his lips to disagree, but Rabbi Shapiro shushed him. "God allowed Deborah to nurture those three babies in her womb for six-and-a-half months."

"Then he ripped them from her womb."

"Listen, Alan, you are free to rage against God over the loss of your children. But deep within you, there will come a time when you will discover the silver lining."

Alan covered his ears. "Stop! Just stop!"

Rabbi Shapiro kissed Alan's forehead and then rose. I'm sorry to have upset you. "Please allow the Community the mitzvah of cooking and cleaning for you during the coming days. Feel free to reach out to me or the Rebbetzin, day or night."

Alan didn't trust himself to speak as he placed his wife's fruit plate and cup of chamomile tea on a tray. He prepared to exit the kitchen.

Rabbi Shapiro cleared his throat. "One more thing, if you don't mind."

Alan turned back to the rabbi. Now what, he wondered irritably.

"If you need me to speak with your family members regarding Justin's death, I can smooth the path."

"Thanks. We'll be fine."

Rabbi Shapiro rose to his feet. "Know my offer has no expiration date. For what it's worth, I believe you did the right thing."

The rabbi embraced him, then left the kitchen. Alan watched him go. Would the rabbi's compassion turn to ashes once he confessed the whiff of relief he'd experienced upon unhooking his baby's breathing tube?

◇◇◇◇◇◇◇◇◇

Over the next seven days, family, friends, and business colleagues came to pay their respects. Alan's wife sat on the sofa, too drugged to fully acknowledge the mourners' presence. The hours he and Deb spent alone together were filled with recriminations. "I could have had Justin if you hadn't taken him off life support," she'd moan.

"We agreed not to let him suffer in his last hours."

"The doctor said he could maybe have survived another week," she protested.

"'Maybe' is a word without dimensions."

She frowned. "All you care about is absolutes."

"Because absolutes are the only reality!"

"But we could have been there for him, like we couldn't be for our other babies."

Alan let out an anguished cry. Deb pulled him to her. "Let's don't fight," she whispered into his straggly hair.

He nuzzled her neck. "I love you."

"I know you do," she murmured.

Chapter 10

SHANA

Shana's captor snickered as he waved a neon green plastic gun in her face. "You really should see a therapist. It can't be normal for a tough reporter to faint at every little thing."

Shana pulled at her shackles. "Like you're normal, nabbing me from the park to cut me up at grandma's house!"

He aimed the gun at the bridge of her nose. Shana's heart pounded through her nostrils. Was the gun filled with acid instead of water? She struggled to block her eyes. He pressed the trigger.

A cold stream of water smacked her face. "You bastard!"

His body tensed. "You recall who I said would be upset if I cut you up?"

Shana knew damn well who—her daughters! But it was safer for her to pretend otherwise. "Your grandmother, duh!"

Her captor's body relaxed. Evidently, she'd confirmed what he wanted to hear.

"I need to apologize," he said, his voice filled with remorse. "Sometimes my emotions scamper like water beetles."

Shana shivered at the visual image. For sure, this guy was wacko. She needed to mine these momentary lulls in his aberrant behavior. She forced her breathing to slow.

"We all freak out sometimes. I forgive you."

He hung his head between his knees. "Thank you," he mumbled.

Her captor's docile behavior proved more frightening than his outburst, especially since she was sitting in a pool of pee. She proceeded with caution.

"Listen, I smell gross. My thighs are chafing. Do you have some wet wipes and clean clothes I can change into?"

In one swift move, he unzipped her khaki skirt and kicked her fallen cell phone to the radiator. Then he finished undressing her, rolled up the clothing, and threw it into the trash can.

Shana's breathing came hard and fast. In an attempt to shield her naked body, she brought her knees to her chest.

"Are you going to rape me?"

Ignoring her question, he grabbed one of three kitchen towels hanging from the oven that sat caddy-corner to them. Then he slipped the towel beneath her buttocks.

Horrified into silence, Shana observed the out-of-body experience unfold.

Her captor rose and secured a mop and pail from the shallow pantry aligning the opposite wall. Then he disappeared into an adjoining room. Shana heard water stream from a faucet.

A moment later, he returned with a filled bucket. The bitter smell of ammonia permeated the kitchen.

"I wouldn't suggest drinking this; it can kill you." He paused, eyeing the windows, which looked painted shut. "So can breathing ammonia in an unventilated area."

Shana gasped!

Chuckling, he strategically moved the bucket just out of kicking reach.

School janitor? Building maintenance? The bitter smell was seeping into her nostrils. "How do you know my daughters' names?"

He heaved open the cracked window above the sink. "Wouldn't you like to know!"

Now he soaked a spider-webbed old mop in the pail, wiping the excess cleaning solution on the pail rim. Then he shoved her body to the far side of the kitchen sink and rigorously mopped the urine puddle. After he washed and towel-dried the floor, he stood back, Shana's captor bent next to her, removed the soaked kitchen towel she was sitting on, and propped a second dry kitchen towel beneath her buttocks.

"Answers trump money, hands down. But let's save that chat for later. I've been an awful host. Bet you're starving."

Holding her breath, Shana nervously waited for the next shoe to drop.

He gestured to a fluted TV tray. "I've made you some breakfast."

Shana's breathing slowed. Her body was still sticky, but at least rape didn't seem to be on their morning menu. That he treated her nude body as invisible might signify he was gay. It could also mean her ancient body was as appealing as a prune. Why did she even care how attractive she looked to him?

She decided to change tactics. "My arms are tingling." "Would you mind unlocking my shackles, first?"

He picked up the tray and turned toward the hallway "Perhaps you'd prefer to eat later."

Even the tingling combined with the ammonia smell could not stop Shana's taste buds from going on high alert as she eyed her captor's retreating body. "Stop!"

He spun around and gave her a dazzling smile. "Give me your daughter's phone number and I'll feed you your breakfast."

"How about you forget the food and release my shackles instead?"

Again, he picked up the food tray and headed towards the hallway door.

"I need to eat!"

He pivoted and threw the plate of eggs in her face. "You think this is a vacation, Bitch? No wonder Zander didn't want to introduce you to his family."

Shana paid no attention to her captor's sly inference that he knew her daughter's husband; she was too focused on tonguing a flying morsel of scrambled egg. She sucked the tiny morsel through pursed lips. Her first bite of food since yesterday.

Her captor swept the wasted food and broken china plate into a dustpan and emptied it in the trash.

"Why must you force me to treat you like an animal?"

Shana closed her eyes and concentrated on breathing through the prickles in her arms. That dinner plate probably was a family heirloom given her when she married. *You're going to be in deep shit with grandma*, she thought gleefully. Shackles or no shackles, she required food and drink to stay alive. To reconcile with her daughters. To celebrate her first grandchild's birth. By now, the police must be searching for her, the girls' phones tapped. If the Answer Man wouldn't give her his answer, she would give him hers. "Sir?" Her voice shook.

He raised his eyebrows at her respectful tone.

"I'll give you my husband's phone number."

Chapter 11

SHANA
JUNE 27, 2018

By playing the *hubby* card, Shana was bluffing. She knew David would need to ponder all options before making a decision. By that time, she could be dead. She debated whether to phone Becca or Rachel. Becca was the obvious choice since Rachel was over six months pregnant. Becca was a take charge person; she'd be on it like honey on toast.

Her captor draped a kitchen towel between her breasts and knees.

"No need," he said.

A buzzer in her brain was screeching red alert, red alert! But Shana's hunger was screeching even louder. "I can give you my daughter's number instead."

"Don't need it."

Shit! *If he knew Rachel and Becca, he already had their phone numbers.*

"You failed the test," her captor was saying. "You were willing to give me, a complete stranger whom you believe unhinged, a family member's phone number. Your personal survival is obviously more important to you than your family's safety. But I knew that from the beginning."

Shana shivered beneath the wet kitchen towel. "What beginning? I don't know you."

He snickered.

Over the years, she'd exposed truths which had enabled the police to clear or convict an infinite number of individuals. Sometimes those truths had even resulted in the conviction of police officers who'd gone rogue.

Black suspects were convicted and incarcerated at five times the rate of whites; thus, she should be able to remember her golden-haired captor. Maybe he'd been a walk-on character in her life as a reporter: a witness, a victim's friend, or a criminal family member.

"I'm sorry. I don't recall ever meeting you."

He smiled. "Let me put you out of your misery."

Shana gasped at a sudden burning urge to go to the bathroom. "The ammonia water gave me a bladder infection!"

Her captor toyed with his pocket knife. "Seriously? Your life is ticking away, and you're complaining about a bladder infection?"

At the moment, this searing pain took precedence over death. "If you loved your grandmother, if there ever was a woman in your life whom you really loved, help me!"

He calmly replaced his knife in its holder and placed it back in his jeans pocket.

"Rachel mentioned it doesn't take much to freak you out."

Shana's jaw dropped. "You know my daughter?"

Her captor left the kitchen, only to return with a physician's medical bag. Shana snickered to herself. A doctor; every Jewish mother's dream.

"Rachel and I have been Facebook friends since she moved to Vegas," he said as he removed a twin set of tiny purple pills from their foil wrapper. "She thinks I'm the cousin of her Cosmetology friend."

Shana grimaced in emotional duress. "That's how you knew my location, where to kidnap me."

She inched back as he approached, but he put a staying hand on her shoulder. Then he pried open her lips and dropped two pills down her throat. As she began to choke, he slowly poured a china cup of cold water down her esophagus.

"I know Becca from her older sister's Facebook pics."

Now Shana's throat and bladder both felt like she'd swallowed a lit cigar. How could her daughters have befriended this creep?

"Is your Facebook picture real?"

Shana's captor plopped back down on the floor beside her and crossed his legs. "Authentic or fake—that was a tricky choice. Ultimately, I chose *authentic*. That's why you're here."

"But I don't do Facebook," she protested, "and I don't know you!"

"All will soon be illuminated."

Shana could feel her anger resurfacing. "What does holding me for fuckin' ransom have to do with me and my girls?"

His lips tightened. "Language." He closed his eyes and laid his palms upward on his lap for what seemed an eternity.

Shana snickered. "Meditation is about inner peace, or did you miss that lesson?"

Her captor's crocodile smile oozed pity.

"You must have Alzheimer's. Less than an hour ago, I assured you ransom had nothing to do with you being here."

She gnawed her mental fingernails on that very possibility. She was about to deliver a stinging retort when he threw a teacup of ice water in her face. The liquid spilled so fast, she gasped for air. He lowered her head between her naked legs. After a moment, he raised her back into a sitting position.

"Why did you do that?" she sputtered.

"Because you're a needy bitch. No more medical emergencies, unless I'm the one to cause them."

Shana's voice rose ten decibels. "Bet your grandmother's going to be real proud of you when she finds out you've added kidnapping to your resume!"

He stared at her coldly. "Grandmother won't give it a second thought. She's dead."

Chapter 12

BECCA

Becca walked into her sister's hospital room; she was watching *Gossip Girl* reruns on her cell phone. Rachel glanced up at her with a hopeful smile. "Did mom come back yet?"

"You know I would have called you."

"I woke up this morning and thought that maybe I'd just had a nightmare."

Becca grimaced. "It was no nightmare."

"She wouldn't wander off like that, no matter how mad she was. No phone, no purse. The drivers here are crazy. Maybe she tried to cross a main street and got hit by a car. Maybe she's lying unconscious in some hospital room!"

"Calm down! You're the one who should have gone into theater instead of me! All this drama isn't good for the baby."

Rachel humphed. "Not even a 'How are you feeling this morning!'"

"You didn't give me a chance to ask!"

"In case you do care, the doctor put me on a 24-hour magnesium drip to make sure I don't experience contractions. Within two seconds, I started feeling flu symptoms. First I was really, really hot, then really, really cold. My chest felt like there was a crate of Mom's old record albums pushing down on me."

"Remember how she donated those record albums to Goodwill when she moved?"

"Mom said you made her give them away," Rachel jokes weakly. "Any word on her?"

Becca shook her head. "I'm sorry you're feeling so sick."

"I feel perfectly fine now that they took it off. Like the drip never happened."

Anguish sliced her heart like a shard of glass. If only their mom's disappearance was a nightmare from which they'd soon awaken.

Rachel pointed to a small plastic container. "I saved a cup of fruit for you from lunch."

Becca rolled her eyes. "Like that's something I'd ever eat."

"You can't just live on mashed potatoes. You've got to start eating healthier."

Becca hugged her chest. "Give me a break. I've stopped eating processed meats. Doesn't Mom comment enough about my diet?"

"Sorry. We just want you to be healthy." Her sister carefully moved her IV pole a couple of inches away from her hospital bed. Then she pat the space beside her.

Becca slipped off her shoes and crawled into bed next to her. Her sister smoothed her hair from her eyes. "How's Dad taking Mom's disappearance?"

Becca snuggled closer. "He's been at the police station all morning, which is why I couldn't get here earlier."

"Why didn't Dad come with you?"

"He's exhausted, so he dropped me off and went back to the hotel. Says he'll be here this afternoon."

Rachel stopped stroking her hair. "I tried calling him on his cell phone but he's not answering. Is there something you're not telling me?"

Becca knew her sister didn't pose that question lightly. As younger sister, Becca was secret keeper of the family. Only once had she ever confided information a sibling or parent had expressly forbidden her to share. She sure wasn't going to start now.

"Hello?" The word was razor-edged.

"There's nothing to hide. If mom doesn't return by 1:00 p.m., Detective Hernandez will do what she promised to do."

"OMG!" Rachel scanned her incoming phone calls from the previous day. "That person who called me yesterday, then hung up? Maybe mom asked them to use their phone. Here it is! Let's call!"

"Maybe we should let the detective follow through on that," Becca said.

"Hell, no. I'm calling now."

"Rachel, wait!"

But Rachel was already clicking in the numbers. Becca could tell by her sister's expression that someone had answered the phone.

"Yes, hello. This is Rachel. Yesterday afternoon, someone from this number called me, then hung up. I didn't recognize the number or area code." Rachel paused. A young woman's voice came through the phone. Then, "So you don't know who could have reached out? What's that? You say you let someone use your phone? By any chance, did you lend your phone to an older woman with blonde hair and purple streaks?"

Rachel clasped Becca's hands, her expression hopeful.

"She told you she tried to call her daughter, but nobody answered. Do you know where the woman went after she left you?"

She was silent as the response came through the phone.

"Okay, well thanks for your help. I appreciate you." She clicked off the phone.

"I immediately answered the phone, why would mom lie?" Rachel mused.

Becca's face felt hot. "Maybe she was embarrassed about abandoning us at the restaurant. She figured we'd be all over her."

"She only thinks about herself. Doesn't care we'd be worried."

Her sister had voiced Becca's own sentiments. Becca's voice quivered. "We might never again have to complain about Mom's selfish behavior if she's not found!"

Rach's voice trembled. "That was horrible of me to say."

Becca wiped the wetness from her eyes. "I know you didn't mean it. What else did you find out?"

"The phone belongs to a young mom. She was walking her baby through the park in a stroller when mom asked to use her phone. She said she was unsure whether to give the phone to her because the woman—mom—looked scruffy, soaked with sweat. But she finally did so. Mom thanked her and went on her way. She was probably trying to locate a park exit."

"Did she say anything else?" Becca asked.

"We've got to find mom!" Rachel attempted to move her body off the bed, then grimaced.

Becca help her reposition herself. "Stop stressing yourself out! There's nothing we can do until one o'clock."

Rachel closed her eyes, placed her palms on her tummy, and did some deep breathing. When she'd calmed down, she pulled out her cell phone and began to type.

Becca rolled her eyes. "Now what?"

"Let's brainstorm what the detective needs to do to find mom."

"I'm pretty sure she doesn't need our suggestions, Rach."

"Makes me feel like we're contributing! Okay, she needs to question employees of shops bordering the Park exits, and also interview police officers at nearby road intersections. Then there's bus drivers and subway operators. Hotel employees."

"Detective Hernandez is going to hate us for pushing our noses in her business, is that what you want?"

"I couldn't care less. Our mother is missing, not hers! Ouch!"

Becca's heart quickened. She reached for the nurse buzzer.

Her sister placed her hand on her arm. "I'm okay, but I'm feeling really tired."

"Let's don't talk about Mom right now," Becca said.

"Mind if we take a nap?"

"You promise to not pull something once I close my eyes?" Becca asked.

"I'll do my best."

As they cuddled together, Becca silently prayed this was one promise her sister would keep.

Chapter 13

SHANA

"Did you kill her?"

Her captor studied her. "You think I'm capable of killing my own grandmother?"

As unhinged as he was, it was definitely a possibility. "*That* is the Question of the Day."

He gestured at the house. "This place has been empty since my dad parked grandma in a nursing home eleven months ago. She died earlier this year. She willed this hoarder's playground to me. I put it on the market a couple of weeks ago. Of course, you were in no condition to notice when you arrived, but there's a *Contract Pending* sign hanging out front. I've already brought everything to a domestic violence shelter, except for a few clothes and cleaning supplies."

Shana's heart was beating heart attack rhythm, and it had nothing to do with her captor's bizarre choice of shelter. "This house is sold?"

"Yep. Appraiser's already been here, as have the new owners. Know what that means?"

She remained silent, praying this was a nightmare from which she'd soon awaken.

Her captor gave her a pitying smile. "No one's coming through this house until final inspection, when the new owners move in."

"When's that?" she asked half-heartedly.

Her captor consulted his watch: one more oddity given his millennial status.

"Monday, May 25 at 9 a.m. Exactly one week from today."

Shana groaned.

Her captor knelt down. "Just you and me for the next seven days."

Vomit spilled from her lips. "I didn't mean to…," she gasped.

His voice was eerily calm as he swatted a wet wipe across her lips and neck. "No problem. By now, I'm used to your bodily liquids."

"Are you going to k-kill me?"

He kissed her forehead. "There you go again, thinking gruesome thoughts."

Shana felt so confused, she couldn't answer.

Her captor pulled a small key—it looked brand new—from his shirt pocket and unlocked her shackles. "Just to show you I'm working in good faith."

Shana winced as her arms fell to her sides. "Why now?"

"A little bird tells me you're not apt to escape in your birthday suit."

She attempted to pick up the kitchen towel, to cover her breasts with that tiny piece of cloth, but her arms fell to her sides, aching from that slight effort. An image of Eve and Adam cowering before God's all-knowing eyes flitted through her mind.

"Why am I here?" she protested, her voice hoarse.

In response, he tied a nylon boy-scout knot around her ankles and tossed her a roll of paper towels. "In case you get cold."

He assembled his cleaning supplies and grabbed the empty food plate.

Then a shocking memory hit and Shana's bowels exploded.

Her captor jumped to his feet. "What the fuck!"

Chapter 14

ALAN
JANUARY 1983

Two weeks after the funeral, Alan's heart had already reverted to stone. Desperate for relief from pain of fatherhood stolen, he retreated into a sixty-hour work week. Electrical engineering was a stern taskmaster; no time for mourning. Each night he'd return home only to once again encounter his wife's sorrowful expression. Oh, the countless nights he had to stifle his fight or flight response! Because he'd never take a violent hand to his wife, Alan would give her a perfunctory hug, and then head back out to "the gym." Truth was, he was too exhausted to exercise following such grueling work hours. Truth was, she knew it.

His wife fell into a great depression. One night after Alan walked through the door, Deb made him sit down at the kitchen table, where a tumbler of root beer was waiting for him.

"We can't pretend our babies' deaths never occurred."

He took a gulp of soda. "You want me to commiserate with you, but I just can't."

"And I can't endure this pain all alone," she lamented.

"Talk to your grief therapist."

"She wants us to come in together."

He stared across the table at the woman he loved. The woman who had borne his dead children. "You're the one who's depressed, not me."

"You numb out by working crazy hours, but grief is going to catch up with you."

Alan was silent.

"Experts say both parents need to go through the stages of grief at losing a baby." She cast her eyes downward. "Babies."

The key word was losing, thought Alan. God had sent an angel to stay Abraham's hand in slaying his son. The rabbi, however, had absolved Alan of slaying his son. Did a newborn's suffering and imminent death change the verdict? This was the answer for which Alan's soul thirsted. But he loved his wife too much to burden her with that question.

"I understand where you're coming from. I'm just not there yet."

"When will you be ready to go there?" she demanded.

"I don't know. Maybe never."

"Experts say the more we push grief away, the more it attacks at the most inopportune moments."

"The experts this, the experts that." He thought about the debilitating depression he experienced during his workday: walking the hallway on the way back from lunch, buckling his pants while getting dressed for work. How his penis had betrayed him by delivering sperm that resulted in three dead babies. Telling himself to "man up" did nothing to relieve his horrible guilt and loss.

"Because they know what they're talking about and we don't!" said Deb.

He kissed her on the crown of her head. "I'll go pick up some Chinese."

She clung to him. "Don't go. Dinner can wait."

He wavered. What if he actually allowed her to share her grief with him? What if he took a baby step in expressing his own grief to her?

"Alan!"

Agh! The words baby step seared his heart, destroying all what ifs. Exposing their wounds would prove too raw for them to absorb without falling into a dark place of no return.

She knocked his tumbler to the floor. "Talk to me, damn it!"

As if in slow motion, Alan watched the pop spill from his glass.

He extricated himself from his wife's arms and stormed out the door.

Alan couldn't deny his feeling of relief as he slid behind the wheel of his Audi GT and clicked on the ignition.

Chapter 15

SHANA

Shana's captor strode toward her, fists clenched. She forced herself to stare him down. Although borne of fear, her gross potty move had bought her a few moments of silence as muddled memories bubbled to the surface. Memories she'd planned to take to the grave with her.

He pulled her up by the hair. "You got dementia, defecating all over the place?"

"What do you think?" she retorted.

Her captor threw a pail of sudsy water at the putrid mess. "I think you're my mother."

Shana fought against the accusation in his words, the same way she fought against the watery goulash he slammed against her thighs. Her ankles still bound, Shana grabbed the radiator in an attempt to raise herself off the floor, but her feet slipped out before her and she fell hard on her haunches.

"It took one foster home and two adoptions to figure it out," he continued bitterly.

Still, she was in denial. "If you really are Facebook friends with Rachel, you'd know she only has a sister."

He sauntered over to the refrigerator freezer, then tossed a bag of ice in her direction. "'Cause Rachel has no clue she's got a brother she's been separated from for three decades," he said bitterly.

Amidst the wet muck, Shana managed to position the ice bag against her tailbone. "Mine was a closed adoption. Those files are sealed."

"So you admit you did give a baby up for adoption," he persisted.

"That may be so, but I know a money scam when I see one."

He scooped a handful of human manure from the floor and held in her face. "If you thought this was a scam, you wouldn't have let loose with your shit."

Shana cringed, considering the implications for her bladder infection. "I lied when I told you my husband could afford to pay your ransom."

Her captor washed his hands in the soapy water. "Tell me something I don't know. If you'd seen my car, you'd know money is the last thing I need. What I want, what I need, is closure. One way or another, you're going to give it to me."

"Closure? What kind of closure?"

Now they were eye-to-eye. "Admit I'm your son."

"You kidnap me, terrorize me, and then have the balls to ask me for closure? No son of mine would ever do this. I hope your birth mother, whoever she is, will be spared this truth."

Her captor's eyes filled to the brim with a reservoir of hurt. Then he spoke.

"My current father? He spared my grandma the truth. He didn't tell her he was putting her into hospice to die, he just told her it was a nursing home. He said the truth would be too traumatic for her to hear."

Shana guffawed at the irony. "You obviously don't care whether your version of the truth will be too traumatic for me and my family to hear."

"Perhaps your opinion of me will change after I share my story."

When Chicago winter temperatures hit eighty degrees, Shana thought wryly.

"When I graduated college, my adoptive parents gave me two gifts. The first gift was a brand new Jeep Cherokee. The second gift was my adoption papers from the Department of Children and Family Services."

"Which gift did you prefer?" she snarled.

The young man's face flushed in anger.

"You are a cruel, misguided individual masquerading as my long-lost son. Out of the goodness of my heart, I will tell you my truth. Thirty-four years ago, I placed a private adoption ad through an attorney. From a handful of offers, I chose a young interfaith couple who held well-paying jobs, as well as a desire to shower their love on a new baby. They were in the hospital room when I delivered."

He tossed her a dry kitchen towel. "Guess where I work."

Shana tossed it back at him. "Before we play guessing games, I need a bath towel."

He rolled the kitchen towel into a ball and threw it at her face. "Where you're going, you won't need a bath."

The implication of his words terrified her, but Shana refused to react as she dried herself with the small towel.

"Department of Children and Family Services. It was the first place I applied. Got hired on the spot."

"Let me repeat. I did private adoption."

"You sure about that?"

"Listen, you've got the wrong person. Just give me some clothes and let me go."

Ignoring her outburst, her captor continued. "I hacked into my DCFS adoption file and reached out to a Linda and Marshall Storkenheim, the couple who adopted me as a newborn infant. Linda was a nurse, her husband was a stockbroker. Recognize their names?"

Shana put her hand to her heart. A coincidence?

"The Storkenheims could have adopted other children from other birth moms."

"Unlikely."

"Why?"

"I was the only child in the house. Linda died in a car accident on my fourth birthday. Both sets of grandparents had passed away, and my first dad didn't feel he could adequately care for me, so he gave me up to DCFS. You should have seen him blubber his way through recounting my story. He begged to reconnect with me now, but that's a non-starter. I'd have to tell him about the negligent foster parents I endured after he gave me up. There's no use him beating himself up for the rest of his life, too."

Shana noticed he hugged himself as he spoke. "Sounds like your adoptive father's a special person."

"They both were. Linda took me to playgroups when I was little. We'd sing and read together all the time. Marshall would take me bird watching—who takes a little kid bird watching, right?"

Shana nodded, grudgingly curious about her captor's early years.

"We went to the nature center a lot; I loved the snake and reptile exhibits. Dad even got me a big boy bed in the shape of a crocodile."

Shana's reporter instinct kicked in. "How come you refer to Marshall as 'Dad,' but your adoptive mom as 'Linda'?"

He raised a fist toward her face. "Understand this. When Linda died, my world ended."

Open mouth, stick foot in, her daughters would say. Only this time, Shana knew she was playing with fire.

"I apologize for questioning your relationship with your adoptive mother. It sounds like she and Marshall loved you very much."

Immediately, her captor's fist opened. Shana noticed his fingers were long and tapered, like her own.

"If you thought I was your birth mother, why wait three decades to contact me?"

Her captor slapped his knees.

"The records indicate you never searched for me. But I was OCD about finding you. I had to ask why you did it. Why you gave me up."

How could her own battered body compare to a lifetime of emotional pain he'd endured. Still, she needed more proof.

"How did you discover my name?"

"Marshall was uncomfortable about invading your privacy, so I traced the microfiche trail—that's all they had in those days—back to the beginning."

Shana placed a restraining hand on his. Her eyes softened as she gazed at her son; his eyes held a speck of green, as did hers. No more denials; this was the baby she'd given up for adoption over three decades ago.

Chapter 16

DAVID

12:00 p.m. David attempted to rouse himself from the luxurious king-sized bed, but the Roosevelt Hotel's 800-thread sheets pulled him back like a passionate lover. Sex was the last thing he should be thinking about when his wife was missing.

He couldn't wrap his head around the fact that his street-smart wife had gone missing. The thing was, Shana exuded an air of competency. When the girls were growing up, she'd scheduled all pediatrician appointments, volunteer experiences, Hebrew school, extracurricular activities, summer camp, and vacations. A grueling amount of activities, in addition to her working as a full-time news reporter.

His wife's refusal to entertain mediocrity, both in her professional and in her personal life, was one of the many character traits that endeared her to him through forty years of marriage. But that determination had caused him many a sleepless night, like the frosty Saturday night she drove her beater through the south side of Chicago in order to rendezvous with an alderman who had secrets of local corruption to share.

Before the kids were born, there'd been even more frightening nights when he'd worked side-by-side her, photographing the sex traffickers, pimps, gang leaders, and police corruption she uncovered. But whether he was at her shoulder or on the other side of town, she always came home to him, all in one piece, laughing away his concerns, assuring him she had everything under control. Which was why her disappearance was so disconcerting.

Still, David was in no hurry to start his day—this first morning without his wife, who was the rudder in his life. He wanted to pretend she had gone on an interview and would return soon. But hell, they were in New York, not North Carolina. Maybe he shouldn't have urged her to leave Chicago in the first place. Maybe he shouldn't have used Rachel's pregnancy as a tool to manipulate Shana to move closer to their daughter and her growing family.

The truth was, now that he was retired, he felt lonely and old. While he loved futzing around with Adobe Photoshop, Canva, and Photomatix Pro, he failed to elicit an enthusiastic response from Shana as he discussed his adventures. She would feign exhaustion after a long day at work and head to bed soon after dinner.

David had hoped Shana would wear retirement like a Tiffany necklace. Instead, their arguments had become a Virginia Wolfe marathon. He wanted more of her time, she still wanted to change the world.

His thoughts landed on infidelity. Had she met someone more exciting? More into wellness and fitness? More charming? Was she not really missing, but with her lover?

These and more troubling questions itched his soul. He debated if he really wanted to discover the answers.

Sure, Shana was no tourist to telling a little white lie. But on the important stuff, Shana valued full disclosure. If she wanted to leave him, she would have come out and said so. His gut told him there was more to her disappearance than met the eye. For example, no matter how intense Shana and the girls' arguments, they would always make up before bed. Shana was a communicator, through and through. It was unlike her to go into shutdown mode, to make them worry.

In fact, except for yesterday's mishap at brunch, Shana had been much calmer around Rachel, due to their daughter's pregnancy. The irony was that worry and stress over her mother's disappearance had caused Rachel's water to break. She could deliver anytime now. Shana must be there to witness the birth. If only he was man enough to go in like Clint Eastwood and shoot the kidnapper. If only he knew the kidnapper's identity. Reality was a bitch.

David reluctantly pushed the bed covers off his body, secured his cane, and headed for the shower. First on today's agenda would be to visit his daughter at the hospital. He prayed both Rachel and the baby were all right.

Chapter 17

ALAN
FEBRUARY 1983

At the rabbi's encouragement, Alan and his wife sat together across from Dr. Ziva Gardner. Deborah's psychiatrist was gently probing about the passing of their three babies.

"Talking about the deaths has enabled me to feel more connected to the babies."

"It sounds like you're saying that naming all three of your children before burying them gave you peace," said Dr. Gardner.

"When people pass away, their souls continue on in the afterlife," explained Deborah. "We want Metushalach and Mahalallel, our stillborn babies, as well as Justin, to be resurrected and reunited with us when the Messiah comes."

Alan noticed the slight blush on his wife's cheeks. It was obvious she, too, was getting something from this encounter with the therapist.

"And the circumcision of all three infants also brought you comfort?"

"We performed these deeds so our babies could die in peace and their souls live on," said Alan. "Even though circumcision is not an obligation and is done without the traditional blessing, we didn't want the babies to suffer the shame of being buried uncircumcised."

"Do you and your wife observe kaddish?"

"The laws of mourning don't apply for a baby that does not live at least thirty days." Alan did not admit it out loud but observing a traditional one-year mourning period would have forced him to acknowledge that the passing of his babies was not merely a nightmare.

The therapist shifted in her chair. "Over the last five months, Deborah has shared with me how her vision of herself has changed after the death of the babies."

Alan stiffened, unsure if his response was required. If so, what response?

Deb must have noticed his discomfort because she took his hand in hers.

The doctor continued. "Your wife has talked about the unparalleled privilege of carrying and nurturing those lives within her womb, feeling creative and complete. Delivering babies dead from her womb causes her to despise her body for its betrayal."

Slivers of his frozen heart begin to crack. "This is a bad idea, me coming here."

His wife moved her chair closer to his. Her face was tearless. How could she not be breaking apart? Perhaps she had already done so in front of this shrink. And now her grief had surpassed his.

"You're sorry you came here tonight?" asked the psychiatrist.

"The wounds are too fresh and raw. I can't do this."

"Your wounds are still too raw too deal with."

Alan couldn't even respond to her rephrasing of his comment. Instead, he resorted, as usual, to communal beliefs. "As tradition teaches, every soul enters this world with a mission. Our babies completed their mission in their time inside the womb and shortly thereafter."

"It is common for bereaved fathers to distance themselves from the feelings of loss they are experiencing," said Dr. Gardner. "To stand back as their wives receive condolences, offers of assistance. This is for her, not for me, they say. Does this resonate with you?"

He sunk into the sofa cushion, feeling weak and dizzy. "Can I have some water?"

As the therapist rose to pour him a glass from her Brita pitcher, Alan glanced at his wife. She looked at him with compassion, for once not attempting to fix his feelings.

Alan sipped from the glass the therapist offered him.

"Before the babies died, I was filled with fresh, molecule-packed water, like the water in this glass. As baby after baby emerged from my wife's womb, as they each died in their own way, that water began to evaporate. When I disconnected Justin from life support, when both sides of our families viewed me and my wife as monsters, my water dried up completely. I became a desert. I am a desert still."

"It is interesting you choose water as your metaphor," said the psychologist. "Water keeps a fetus alive in the womb. It delivers nutrients, it provides a soft barrier, it is everything to that fetus until a baby emerges. Do you feel responsible for the death of your babies?"

His wife breathed in harshly.

Alan put his head in his arms. His mask was disintegrating, and he could do nothing to paste it back on. He was helpless.

Deb took him in her arms. "It's all right," she cooed over and over again. He was in her womb, unconditionally loved by his wife, by God, by the therapist. He was finally home.

"There will be times when you will feel you can't survive the pain. Don't chastise yourselves by saying if only we'd done this, if only we'd done that. Instead, cling to God and each other, talk to each other. You are both resilient; you will come through this together."

As Alan paid for the therapy session, he felt lighter than he'd felt in months. It was as if bricks and mortar had come undone. Angels' wings carrying him and Deb out of the therapist's office and into the street. Never had he felt this loosening of should and shouldn't.

Before slipping into the driver's seat, Alan gave his wife a hug filled with the love and passion he'd held hostage within his heart. He prayed his heart would remain open.

Chapter 18

SHANA

"You are my son."

The young man's eyes grew wide.

"When I found out I was pregnant with you, I was ecstatic, but also freaked out!"

He raised his eyebrows. "Afraid I was a monster?"

Afraid your birth father was a monster. Shana kept that response tightly tucked away in her head.

"Of course not. I'd just been offered a job as a newspaper writer; heady stuff for a new college graduate. No way could I take care of another human being when I didn't even know if I could take care of myself. I didn't know what to do, who to turn to."

"I should be glad you didn't abort me," he said, his voice at once solemn.

"My parents were hippies. They told me it was my personal choice whether to give birth or abort. I chose to bring you into this world. Thanks to the Pregnancy Discrimination Act, the Sun-Times had to keep me on staff, even as my belly grew bigger and bigger with you."

"Who is my father?"

Shana's hunger banged on her gut. "No more talk until you give me food and clothes."

He turned his back on her. "You're pretending to care about me so I'll release you."

Shana softened her tone. "I'm not pretending, Daniel."

Caught off guard, he turned to face her. "That was my birth name."

"I know," she said quietly. "The Storkenheims let me name you. That name also worked in Hebrew when they had you circumcised."

Shana watched her son's eyes flicker.

"I'll get you some food and clothes." He strode from the kitchen.

Shana was left with her own dark thoughts. Never had she mentioned to Rachel and Becca that they had a long-lost sibling she'd given birth to out of wedlock. She couldn't even recall confiding in David, although they'd recently celebrated their fortieth wedding anniversary. What if the family spit her out of their lives, like bitter herbs?

Vulnerability was an emotion Shana had studiously avoided her entire life. As an only child, she'd been forced to be self-reliant at an early age. Her parents were more focused on their next LSD trip than in caring and feeding a young child. At eight years old, Shana had set their apartment ablaze while frying eggs in an ungreased pan. Most kids would have run screaming from the kitchen, but not her. Without batting an eye, she'd turned off the stove jets, then thrown a pitcher of water at the fire. A pale scar on her right forearm was a constant reminder of the pain she had endured.

As far as Shana was concerned, she'd also done a hell of a job being a good wife and mother. Even so, there was a huge difference between confiding almost everything about your past and confiding every single thing! How could she expose her daughters to a sibling who was so fucked up? Maybe the Ecstasy drug her rapist put in her drink had resulted in her son's mental illness, or maybe he was simply born evil. Since Judaism didn't believe in original sin, the second possibility was a non-starter. Whatever his problem, the fact remained that her son had kidnapped her and held her captive. Who knew what else he was capable of doing?

Daniel reappeared with an armful of clothes. "Here you go," he said, his voice subdued.

"Thank you." She quickly slipped into some undergarments and a dress that smelled of moth balls. "So what's your new name?"

He waved his hands agitatedly. "Later."

Shana adopted a soothing tone of voice. "The Storkenheims loved you. I love you, too."

Daniel plated some fresh eggs and toast and handed her the food. "Obviously not enough to search for me."

As Shana stuffed scrambled eggs and jam into her mouth, she mulled the resigned tone of his words. "Search is an interesting word choice, Daniel."

"I told you no games." His voice was low and threatening.

Fear crawled up Shana's spine like a thousand red ants. "You scaled mountains to search me out. I failed to search for you because I knew I'd given my precious baby to a loving, financially secure, couple. Right now, I'm overwhelmed with both positive and negative emotions."

He snickered. "Guilt is a bitch."

"Guilt is not one of those emotions," she whispered.

His head jerked up. "You started a new life and pretended I never existed!"

Shana breathed deeply, afraid to set him off again. "I yearned to see you. But I've interviewed numerous birth parents who re-enter their children's lives. The results are often crushing. In some cases, the children didn't even know they were adopted. I didn't want you and your adoptive family to experience that tsunami upheaval."

He hit her elbow with his fist. "You worked for the newspaper less than a year when you had me; you didn't know all that stuff when you discarded me. Face it. You chose to erase me from your life like an old Etch a Sketch pad. To protect yourself, not me."

Shana winced as she rubbed her elbow. "What do you want from me?"

He smashed her empty plate against the kitchen wall. "I want thirty-four years of my life back. I want memories of foster care and beatings and neglect erased. I want to know my birth family. To meet my siblings. To break free of the shadows in my life."

"In between the first adoption and your current adoption, you were placed in foster care?"

Daniel looked away. "I acted out; biting, scratching, hitting."

Tears flowed down Shana's cheeks. "You were a preschooler. You needed love and affection, not beatings and neglect."

"I never said they beat me."

"Then what did they do to you?"

"It wasn't just me. There were other kids there, too."

"What did your foster parents do?" Shana repeated.

"They collected checks and used them to buy lavish meals while feeding us watery soup and moldy bread."

"Like *Oliver Twist*," she mused.

"They tied us to our bed railings at night so we wouldn't run away."

"So that's why you shackled my wrists."

Daniel's eyes glowed fiercely. "You know nothing about me. You gave up that opportunity thirty-four years ago."

Shana willed herself to stay calm. The police would be looking for her by now. The longer she kept him talking, the longer she'd stay alive. "Did your preschool teacher report your abuse to DCFS?"

"Some lady with a clipboard came to our house a couple of times. But our foster parents threatened us not to answer her questions or we'd be beaten. Some of us had red marks around our wrists and ankles, but we all wore long sleeves and pants, and the lady didn't notice."

"How awful," said Shana. "How were you finally removed from their care?"

"The weather was scorching hot. The lady with the clipboard forced our foster parents to have us roll up our sleeves and pants and take off our shirts. Our ribs had no fat on them, and our wrists and ankles were infected. DCFS got us out of there quick."

Shana huffed. "Wish I would have covered that story. I'd make them pay for what they did to you and the others."

Daniel hit her on the arm. "Don't you get it? You caused the story!"

Shana winced as she rubbed the injury. "I wish I could erase those horrible foster care experiences from your brain, Daniel, but you must realize I had no control over your early childhood."

He smirked. "How convenient for you."

Her voice reflected his grief. "I am so sorry."

His fists tightened. "Crocodile tears. No matter. You're not much longer for this world."

Shana trembled. Her life was in the hands of her emotionally unstable son. She must convince him to release her. She'd soon be a grandmother for the first time. But how could she exit this nightmare when her feet were roped like a prized calf? All hope was lost unless she gave Daniel the acceptance he craved.

"Let me text your sisters. Tell them where we are, not to bring the police. They'll be thrilled to meet you."

He advanced towards her. "Don't bullshit a bull-shitter, Mommy!"

"Untie this rope, open the door, send me back into the woods," she pleaded. "I promise I won't tell anybody."

He pulled a chair from the kitchen table and pushed her into it. His eyes had steadied. "You haven't told me about my birth father yet."

Chapter 19

RACHEL

Sweaty, chilled, nauseous, head pounding. Rachel could only bear the second day of magnesium drips because it strengthened her baby's lungs in utero. And because her dad had assured her and Becca that Detective Hernandez and the NYPD were out there, trying to find their mother.

Limp as a wilted leaf, she lay in her hospital bed, praying not to go into premature labor. Time, said the doctor, was the most important gift she could give her unborn infant. Time for the lungs, time for the organs, time for the brain, to develop. Each additional moment enabled the baby to safely grow inside her drained womb; that's what the nurse had said.

The goal was no contractions; even light ones could stress the baby. Her doctor wanted her to continue on bed rest for at least ninety-eight more days; until the baby was further equipped to live outside utero. They told her she needed to remain calm, because her anxiety would transmit to the fetus.

Rachel tried to remain calm. She listened to Chopin and Bach on her iPhone. Zander massaged her neck and shoulders. Becca snuggled and played board games with her. But when her family left for the cafeteria, anxiety over her mom's disappearance encased her brain. It's your fault. You're responsible. A truth she couldn't deny.

If only she could rerun the last three days of her life, like the movie *Ground Hog Day*. She'd smile at her mom from across the brunch table. When her mom asked the waiter to turn down the air conditioning, she'd second that request; after all, it had been cold in the restaurant.

She'd generously hand her mother a sweater, sans snarky comment. When her mother rushed from the dining room, obviously embarrassed by her daughters' behavior, she'd not follow dad's suggestion to "give mom a minute."

If mom wasn't in the bathroom, she'd check out the bar, the hostess desk, the outside patio. She'd refuse to pretend like nothing was amiss.

If she'd done all that, mom might be sitting on her hospital bed, singing to her right now. Beatles songs. Carole King. James Taylor. Songs from mom's youth. Songs she'd exposed her daughters to when they were young. Songs of peaceful uprising and change.

Then the brutal truth wedged itself into her thoughts. If she had been more compassionate toward mom, she wouldn't even be lying in the hospital right now. Her water wouldn't have broken. She would have delivered her baby on her due date!

It was her own fault.

Rachel sobbed like she had when 9/11 happened. Even though she was just a freshman at a Chicago high school, she'd intuited what New York's twin towers symbolized. What their destruction symbolized.

That day, Mom returned home early from work. She rocked her and her younger sister. Ran her fingers through their hair. Allowed them to cry. To freely experience their sadness.

"Reality consists of joy and horror," she'd said. "We must be strong enough to live through them both."

Now mom's words were playing out again. If the police didn't find her soon... she couldn't think about that.

She must have been sobbing louder than she thought. Suddenly she felt a sharp contraction and pressed the alert button. Seconds later, nurses rushed into the room, checked her IV, her heart monitor, and then the baby's heart monitor and brain activity.

Rachel felt a pin prick in her arm. "This will calm you down," the nurse said gently.

"The baby!"

"Your baby is fine for now, but she requires a stress-free environment to develop inside your womb. Agitation can cause contractions. You could go into premature labor, which would have a negative impact on your baby."

Rachel swiped at her eyes. "Sorry. It's just everything. And my mom not being here."

The nurse pat her hand. "Right now, you need to concentrate on your health and that of your baby. Your mom would want that, right?"

Rachel nodded. The medicine was making her sleepy. She closed her eyes.

Mom would want that.

Chapter 20

SHANA

Shana debated what to do. If she told Daniel the truth about his birth father, she'd be a goner. If she didn't talk, odds were he'd still kill her.

The pocketknife in her face decided for her. "Start talking."

Shana breathed in and out deeply, then stuck one toe into the mire.

"I majored in Journalism at Roosevelt University. Back in the day, the newspaper world was still dominated by men. Sexism was still a big part of women not being hired and promoted. Then there's the salary disparity and …"

"Birth father, not politics!"

A lucid speaker, Shana had rarely encountered a No-Fly zone.

"I met your dad at a frat party a week before graduation."

Daniel leaned in. "Where?"

Shana thought a minute. "The frat house was in an old mansion."

Her son waved his knife at her. "What was the name of the fraternity?"

Shana hugged her trembling body. "I don't remember. That was thirty-five years ago!"

"Go on."

"He was a hotty, as we used to call cute guys. Tall, well-built, dark hair, green eyes."

"What was his name?"

This time she shielded her face in her hands. "I don't know."

He forcefully lifted her chin. "No more games!"

"I was drunk," she pleaded. "We danced to Saturday Night Fever! Sweaty. Music pounding. Strobe lights on the dance floor making my head hurt. I left my drink at the bar and stumbled to the bathroom. When I came back, he'd gotten refills for us both. Next thing I know, I was sprawled on a bed. Alone. Naked. Sun streaming into the room."

"Shame on you, copping a *Me Too* experience!"

"Political figures and celebrities aren't the only rapists, Daniel."

"Did you report it? That's what you advise date rape victims to do."

Her eyes widened.

He snickered. "I've read quite a few of your newspaper stories, Mommy."

Shana stared into her son's eyes. "I didn't report your father, Daniel. In those days, women who were sexually assaulted were made to feel like criminals."

"Nothing's changed there," he scoffed.

She stared at him. "You seem to know a lot about the subject."

He wasn't biting. "You package bogus advice in neon gift bags."

Despite her emotional pain at revealing the sordid events leading to her pregnancy, Shana couldn't help but admire Daniel's visual imagery. Her thoughts began to drift; perhaps her son could be a writer, or a poet. She could see him now, standing before hundreds of people eager to hear every uttering of this talented wordsmith.

Snip. Snip.

Shana whirled around to find a handful of purple and blonde hair lying on the floor by her feet. Her hand went to the back of her head. "What did you do?" she shrieked.

"Helping you refocus."

"I want out of here, you son of a bitch!"

"So you finally admit you're a bitch!"

"If you don't release me, I'll shit all over the floor again," she threatened.

Daniel shrugged. "That's your choice. FYI, we're out of paper towels, and the ammonia bottle is empty, so...."

Shana began picking at the skin on her arms. "What do you want?"

"Finish your story, and I'll let you go."

She willed her breathing to slow. "The advice I offered rape victims was not the advice I received when it happened to me. I felt like a used condom, but my parents were too stoned to offer me anything more than a peace necklace."

Daniel broke out into a guffaw. "You paint great pictures with your words!"

Shana raised her eyebrows.

Daniel turned solemn. "Were you a virgin when you had sex with my father?"

The fact that she had been a virgin at the time of the rape. "My prior sex life has nothing to do with the fact that your father drugged and raped me. I did not give my consent to have intercourse with him. He took what he wanted and left."

"Like Robin Hood."

"Nothing like Robin Hood."

"Did you tell your friends, your teachers, anybody besides grandma and grandpa?"

Hearing her son refer to her parents as his grandma and grandpa was absurd. When she'd gone into labor, they'd been so zoned out, her best friend drove her to the hospital.

Now he was in her face. "What's so damn funny?"

As a reporter, Shana had demonstrated the cunning of a jaguar; planning, foreseeing her opponent's every move. But her captor's continuous mood changes had reduced her to a hamster running on a wheel.

Confusion burst through her consciousness; the confusion she'd seen in veterans with PTSD. She had to try one more time to get through to him. "Do you take medication, Daniel?"

He looked away. "Not your business."

Shana attempted to calm her breath, breathing in and out slowly. "My dad was bi-polar. He smoked marijuana and took LSD to self-medicate. He hung himself when he was forty-nine years old. I don't want that for you."

Her captor jumped to his feet and pulled his knife on her. "Enough!"

Shana's eyes widened as the singing blade threatened to sting her carotid artery.

Chapter 21

DAVID

With the hullabaloo over Detective Hernandez's non-evidence summary, David hadn't gotten a chance to talk privately to his girls about what concerned him most. Rachel had mentioned the nurses and doctor were in and out of her room all morning, so he planned an afternoon visit.

When David meandered into the room around noon, cane in hand, Rachel was in the bathroom and Becca was already chowing down, if you considered kale and endive salad with pecans and mandarin oranges to be an actual meal.

"Hey, Daddy," said Becca. "Want some of my salad? I'm trying to eat healthy."

Leaning on his cane, David bent down to kiss her on the cheek and got a smidge of honey mustard dressing on his lips.

"Thanks, but no thanks. These days, my stomach and raw greens are at a stand-off."

His younger daughter grinned. "I'm no great salad fan, either, but I promised Rachel I'd give it a try."

"They bring that salad to the room?"

She nodded. "Rachel ordered it for me," she said in-between forking orange slices into her mouth. "Want something to eat, daddy? I can grab you something from downstairs after I'm done eating."

David waved off Becca's concern—a gesture that drove his wife crazy. *You never let me do anything nice for you, and then you call me selfish,* she'd say. He yearned to hear her words of concern for him right here, right now. "I'll run down to the cafeteria later."

His daughter chuckled. "You're so funny."

David attempted a high, squeaky voice. "What did I do now?"

"You said 'run.' You can barely walk."

He hung his head in mock chagrin. "Next time I'll be more exact with my verbiage."

She giggled. "See that you do!"

David placed his cane against the wall and took a seat opposite his daughter. "So, how's your big sister feeling today?"

Rachel shuffled out of the bathroom. "I'm right here, Dad. I can answer for myself."

David's face lit up at sight of his older daughter. "How's my princess doing today?"

She carefully hugged him and maneuvered herself back into her bed. "Much better, thanks. They unhooked the IV magnesium drip before you got here, so no more IV pole, thank goodness! But having to wear these support hose so I don't get a blood clot is annoying."

Becca grimaced. "Better than the alternative. Want me to prop your bed so you can eat?"

Rachel pressed the button. "Got it. Thanks, though."

David grimaced. His younger daughter was solicitous, just like Shana. But Rachel was fiercely independent, just like him; they both abhorred being fussed over. No indication Becca felt slighted by her sister's response, though. Unlike his wife, she didn't take it personally. She was more self-confident, while Shana required constant confirmation of her self-worth, especially in the months since she'd retired from the Newspaper.

"Bec," said Rachel, "can you please pump some hand sanitizer on a paper towel for me?"

Becca put aside her food tray and sprang from her chair.

"I could have gotten it," said David. "Your sister is still eating."

Both girls locked eyes from across the room. His eyes burned as he read the unspoken message between them. It would take him at least five minutes to accomplish even that simple mobility task. First he'd have to push himself out of the chair—three tries was the charm. He'd grab for his cane, and then shuffle over to the sink, one step at a time. By the time he completed the task, Rachel would be finished eating.

As Rachel wiped down her bedside table with the moist paper towel, David switched topics. "What did the doctor say about the baby?"

"Her heartbeat's strong, thank God. They're giving me an ultrasound today to make sure her lungs and organs are developing as they should. Any new updates on mom yet?"

"The detective has contacted all the park vendors to see if anyone noticed a person with an oversized black umbrella and alligator shoes before it began to storm."

"Yesterday, she said everybody left the park when the weather got bad," said Becca.

Rachel used her finger to scrape up the last bit of lettuce on her plate, then pushed her bedside table aside. "A lot of people probably brought their umbrellas to the park Sunday."

"The weatherman said sunny and hot all day," said Becca. "If the skies are clear, you're not going to cart a big umbrella along."

Rachel put her feet on the floor, and then stepped into her slippers. "Some cultures use umbrellas to guard against the sun."

Becca placed her hands on her hips. "Okay, Miss Know-it-all!"

"Okay, Miss Sold-it-all," teased Rachel.

"Okay, Miss Sang-it-all," retorted Becca.

"Okay, Miss Olang Sang Ruby Institute all," countered Rachel.

David laughed along with his daughters. Overnight camp had been a joyful time for his daughters, as well as a welcome respite for him and Shana. It had been a month of eating at whatever time they chose, making food choices the kids hated, exploring wine vineyards and going dancing at midnight without having to worry about where the kids were. It was great to reconnect with each other after months of operating on autopilot with everybody's crazy schedules. Engaging in sex without fear the kids would burst into their bedroom at any minute, complaining of upset stomachs or nightmares.

In later years, when the girls were engaged as camp counselors for the whole summer, he and Shana would use their accumulated vacation and personal days to splurge on annual couple cruises they'd arranged a year prior.

Those vacations had made both of them giddy. But try as they might, once they got home, the intensity of their renewed love would fade within a week or two. Soon, they'd begin bickering about who was doing what chore and who was driving what child to basketball or drama. When his health went to shit, that had added money to his wife's list of complaints.

"Where do you think you're going, Rach? The doctor said you're not allowed to get out of bed except to go to the bathroom."

"Hawaii!" joked Rachel.

"But you and Zan have already been there."

Rachel snapped her fingers. "Exactly!"

"Exactligh."

"Exactlow."

"Exactpee!"

"Stop!" Rachel giggled. "You're making the baby kick!"

"Silly mommy and auntie," said David.

"Come on, Daddy," said Becca. "I'll walk you down to the cafeteria."

"For a minute, I thought you were asking me to walk you down the aisle!" he joked.

"You already did that with Rachel," she teased.

David attempted to rise from his chair, but his body was unwilling. It took him a couple of tries, but he was finally able to extract his credit card from his wallet without first standing. "Go yourself. Get me a cheese sandwich and chocolate ice cream. I'll stay with your sis."

"Thought you have high cholesterol?" Becca asked.

"Don't tell Mom," he kidded.

Both girls' faces dropped.

"Sorry," he whispered.

Rachel inched toward the bathroom. "Walking is good for you, Dad."

"Leave Daddy alone, Rach. He doesn't want to go, and that's that."

"I'm just a stubborn old bastard, that's what Mom always…"

Shit. Shana's disappearance was turning him inside out and upside down.

Becca grabbed his credit card and headed into the hallway.

Chapter 22

SHANA

"You can open your eyes now."

Shana forced herself to do so, unsure if she was still alive.

Daniel replaced the pocketknife in its sheath, then smiled down at her.

"It's been a long morning. Don't know about you, but I'm ready for a nap."

She was dumbstruck. One second her son's knife was at her throat, the next he's talking nap time.

Daniel pulled two neon pacifiers from his pocket; he tossed the turquois one to her. Too shocked to reach for it, she let it drop.

"Suit yourself. This thing helped me quit smoking, saved my life. Relieves anxiety without …."

"You promised to let me go once I told you about your birth father," Shana whimpered. "What more do you want from me?"

Daniel retrieved the fallen pacifier and gently placed it in her lap. "You're overwrought. A nap will help you think more clearly."

"Your father raped me, that's all there is to tell," she screeched.

Shana's captor leaned down to clap her cheeks. "And I'm your avenging angel."

Her hand flew to her face and she gasped. Was this just one more mind game, or did Daniel actually plan to kill his birth father?

Now he presented her with a blown-up air mattress. "Sorry, but I can't provide you with any sheets, in case you choose to adopt my grandma's exit plan. Rest well. FYI, I'm not going to re-shackle your arms this time."

Shana felt the familiar adrenaline rush. "You're certain I won't figure out a way to cut the rope around my calves and escape?"

Daniel looked at her with compassion. "You're welcome to try, but BTW, your success is unlikely. While working in cyber security, I developed a childproofing app that parents can operate without being in close physical proximity to their child."

So he was in cyber security, after all, Shana mused. But the black medical bag and his haste in ministering to her medical needs made zero sense when his compassion was followed by torture.

"You employed your app before coming back into the kitchen," Shana said, disheartened.

Her son chuckled as he knelt to tighten the Nylon knot around her ankles. "No denying I inherited my brains from you! Just to clarify, all kitchen cabinets, drawers, doors beneath the sink, as well as food pantry, stove, and refrigerator, have been secured."

Then he rose to his feet. "Rest well. I'll be asking for a full report on how the pacifier worked for you. Don't let me down."

Shana flung the turquoise pacifier across the kitchen.

Then she rolled onto the air mattress and shut her eyes.

Chapter 23

BECCA

Rachel had shed her hospital gown between hot flashes and was now shivering beneath three blankets. She said her chest felt heavy again, but the nurse assured her that all these symptoms were normal side-effects of the magnesium drip. At least Rachel was not experiencing any contractions. The nurse gave her another shot of steroids in each booty cheek, which artificially speeds up the baby's lung development, just in case the baby was as stubborn as her mother and broke free from the womb.

Dr. Nayman came in to check on Rachel, and said she and the baby were doing fine. She reminded Rachel to stay off her feet, except to go to the bathroom. Then she exited the hospital room.

Becca pulled a chair up to her sister's bedside. Rachel pressed the elevate button for the bed, and then swung her cleared breakfast table over her sheets. "What do you got?"

Today, she'd brought a couple of their favorite board games. Their dad used to play *Chutes & Ladders* with them, but to this day, Mom preferred *Trouble, Parcheesi,* and *Chinese Checkers*, which they played at their weekly get-togethers. Mom laughed her head off when she won; a rare occurrence since Rachel was the board game wizard in the family.

"Are you okay with playing an acting game first?" Becca asked. In the acting class she taught, Becca had her students adopt the poses of various animate objects. She personally found rocks to be the most challenging; although composed of a solid mixture of several minerals, they remain in constant flux. Water wore them down, bit by bit, year after year, smoothing their sharp edges. If Mom were here, Becca would tease her about smoothing her edges! She'd retort, "If I was a rock, I couldn't nuzzle your neck!" Becca swiped at my teary eyes. It's all about Mom.

Rach snickered. "What acting game can I possibly play from bed?"

"Let's pretend we're sea urchins."

"Can I pretend I'm the *Little Mermaid* instead?"

"Little pregnant Mermaid."

"Arielle wasn't so young when she fell in love with the prince!"

"True."

"It's not like he was a pedophile," she joked.

"So not funny."

"And why are we playing sea urchins and Little Mermaid?"

"Because laughter relieves pain."

Rach grasped her throat. "So dry."

Drama queen! Becca refilled her Styrofoam glass; the clear stream of water bounced off melting ice cubes.

Her sister sipped the water. "Thanks. Mind if we just play board games, instead?"

"Whatever." Becca sighed as she removed *Trouble* from its box.

"It's just that mom and I used to play Little Mermaid when I was little."

Becca giggled. "Mom *is* a Little Mermaid."

Rach swiped a tear from her eye. "Mom took me to see the original movie when I was four years old. It was my favorite. We used to sing those songs together all the time. She and Dad even bought me an Arielle dress."

Becca grimaced. "Because you were the favorite child."

"Because you weren't born yet! I remember how Mom and I took tap dancing classes together when she was eight months pregnant with you. I miss her sooo much."

Becca reached in for a hug when her cell rang. "Hey, Dad. Great! See you soon!" She clicked off the phone.

"Why didn't you let me say hi?"

"He was in a hurry."

"Is he on his way over?"

"Soon."

Rachel's eyes grow wide at the lilt in her sister's voice. "Did they find Mom?"

"Not yet."

Her flu-like symptoms had vanished. "What's going on?"

Becca smiled ear to ear. "Dad put up a 'Go Fund Me' page and a Facebook posting."

"Why?"

"We're offering a $20,000 reward for information on Mom's whereabouts."

"OMG!" She pulled it up on her iPhone. "Here it is!"

Excitement flooded the hospital room. "Guess what else?" Becca asked.

"What?"

"The posting and page went up ten minutes ago and Detective Hernandez has already received a couple dozen possible sightings!"

Rachel shared Dad's post through IM. "But what if we don't raise $20,000?"

"We will," Becca said, sharing Dad's Facebook post.

"We should contact the *NY Times* and have them do an article on Mom," mused Rachel.

"Dad's already on it."

Her sister looked up from her phone. "Really?"

"Really!" said Becca. Their dad was the quietest, most passive guy one could ever meet. Mom basked in the attention of others, while dad preferred solitary pursuits like reading about esoteric subjects nobody cares about.

To Becca, his ability to break out of his shell and take charge of this situation after forty years of marriage proved that people can change if their desire is fierce enough. That it took Mom's disappearance to make that change happen was unfortunate.

Rach frowned. "What if Mom doesn't want to be found?"

Becca sloughed off her sister's concern. "Don't be a Debbie Downer!"

But Becca can felt doubt unpack its suitcase. What if their final memory of mom was her fleeing the restaurant after being humiliated in front of Zander's family? That would be a memory from which she and her sister could never recover.

Chapter 24

SHANA

"Time for your pills, Sleepyhead."

Shana smiled in her sleep. "Just a couple more minutes, David."

The tantalizing smell of fresh coffee wafted past her nose, then a kiss on her forehead. David's daily parting gifts to her as he strolled off to his photography studio.

Oh, how she loved being retired. Traipsing into David's studio at lunchtime with TV trays bearing bowls of chicken soup or Cesar salad. Poring over pictures he'd developed using old school techniques. "The new technology doesn't feel quite authentic to me," he'd say.

In their early days of parenthood, Shana would rail against David for spending his evenings in that damn studio, away from the kids. "I get to see you, on-and-off, all day, but the kids miss playing with you after dinner."

"Who reads to them every night?"

"You do," she'd admit.

"Who takes them skateboarding and to the movies on weekends?"

"You do."

"Huh. So I'm not such a bad dad after all," he'd tease.

"Time to get up." This time the voice sounded like tinkling glass.

Shana sat up in bed and rubbed her eyes. "What's the rush?"

He slipped the two purple pills through her chapped lips. "Oh, nothing."

Shana's eyes flew open.

"I trust your air mattress was comfortable?"

She gasped.

Daniel laughed as he put a half-filled cup of water to her lips. "And a good morning to you, too!"

She greedily swallowed the bit of water, and he yanked the cup away.

Then his voice turned businesslike. "Drink your coffee. Your oatmeal will be ready in a second. We need to fortify you to get you through the day. It's going to be a long one."

He turned on his heel and exited the kitchen.

Shana didn't realize she'd been holding her breath. Now she exhaled in one fell swoop. She was so thirsty, she gulped the boiling coffee, cringing as it scalded her throat and gut. What difference did it make? She'd be dead soon. Her family was obviously not looking for her, not even David. His quiet betrayal hurt her the most. She'd always thought he had her back. The girls were right. She really was naive.

Her captor returned, bearing a tray of oatmeal and toast, complete with milk, butter, and a plastic spoon and fork. "Sorry. Couldn't take a chance with giving you a knife. The back of the spoon should work fine, though."

Breathing in the heady smell of apples and cinnamon almost made Shana swoon. She tore into the food with her plastic utensils.

Daniel smiled. "I'm glad you are more amenable today. For your positive change of attitude, you receive a reward."

"Reward?" Shana asked as she continued to feed her face.

"Obviously you never taught kids with behavior disorders. If you had, you'd know that positive reinforcement for deeds well done works on a token system. I accumulated more tokens than anybody else in my classes because I knew how to perform for optimal results."

So he had been in special education, thought Shana.

"For example, Ms. Spaulding, my eighth-grade English teacher, valued well-written prose, so I turned in award-winning prose. A couple of my short stories even went on to state finals! A chip off the old block, right?"

Shana winced.

"But when it came to behavior, another kid's taunting could push me into the deep end. One time I almost choked a bully to death. I thought I was doing humanity a great service, but the school principal disagreed; she suspended me for three days. My adoptive parents—the most recent pair—were disappointed in me. But they never stopped advocating to right my world. They even convinced the principal to knock off one day off my suspension. Big deal."

Shana willed him to continue. The longer her captor remained invested in sharing his story, the less likely an unexpected mood change would result in a violent act; that's what she'd discovered years ago when a criminal suspect she'd been interviewing had taken her hostage.

"Because of my talent in writing, Ms. Spaulding believed I could become a great writer. My interest was in computer technology, but I let Ms. Spaulding think her idea was spectacular.

"I also reined myself in when it came to committing felonious acts. In eighth grade, murder was often on my mind; nothing to do with my adoptive parents, and everything to do with kids saying and doing cruel things to me."

Listening to her son's words, Shana couldn't help but feel his emotional pain.

"Did your teachers or school principal do anything to stop the bullying? These days it's even worse, with cyber bullying and…." She'd been about to add and on-line stalking until she realized that's exactly what he'd done to her daughters.

Would her son read her mind? Guess how she'd been poised to end that sentence, as well as its implications? At this point, she believed he could do just about anything he put his mind to, which scared her to hell. She held her breath in anticipation of a punishment.

Evidently, he was too intent on recounting his story to even notice she'd ceased talking mid-stream.

"Ms. Spaulding and I worked out a behavioral reinforcement program for me. Every time an angry feeling burst into my head, I raised my index finger. There were times I wanted to raise a different finger, but I refrained. During class lectures, my teacher would meander by and drop a token on my desk. Ridiculous, huh? Working for a paper token?"

Shana thanked God for allowing her to bypass that bullet. She'd never been super religious, but at times like this, she knew in her gut it was more than blind luck.

"Your teacher's praise meant a lot to you," she murmured.

"Sometimes I'd be ready to lose it. I'd stare up at the ceiling. Ms. Spaulding would notice and drop two tokens on my desk. This made me feel like I had the power to control my escalating emotions.

"Ms. Spaulding shared my positive behavioral reinforcement plan with the other teachers, and it began to work; my behavior improved in all of my classes. But there were still times when my pot boiled over. Ms. Spaulding would clear the students from the classroom while I knocked plants and file holders off the back tables. The desks and chairs were nailed to the floor, which frustrated me, but saved my school a ton on repair costs.

"At those times, Ms. Spaulding would silently sit at her desk until my rage subsided. Then she would come sit by my side, look me in the eyes, and tell me I, alone, had the power to control my behavior. She told me she had confidence in me, that I could do it.

"Soon afterwards, I was suspended again, this time for a week. My parents couldn't get me out of that one. Ms. Spaulding wasn't mad. She told me progress is two steps forward, one step back, and repeat. When somebody believes in you, that's the biggest token of them all."

Shana grimaced. Despite her attempt to fend off emotion at any cost, guilt had finally inched its way into her heart.

She'd been there for her daughters. She should have been there for her son.

Daniel continued talking. "The psychiatrist tinkered with my meds and dosage and my life did improve over the next few years. But when I was sixteen, I beat up a teacher who was making racist comments about a classmate. The school put me in anger management classes."

When he paused, Shana asked, "Where do you think all your anger came from?"

"From you abandoning me," he spat, his voice high pitched like a young child.

"Yeah, I get that. Where else?"

Daniel stood abruptly. "No more talk." He toted her empty plate and coffee cup into another room. He soon returned with a green garden hose and connected it to an electrical outlet located above the kitchen counter.

"What's the water hose for?" Shana asked.

"We're going on a field trip. You need to clean yourself."

Her eyes widened. He couldn't be serious. "But the water will flood the kitchen!"

"The sink faucet doesn't work. You'll need to bend over the sink and spray yourself down!"

Shana shuddered. "The water will be freezing. And what about soap?"

"Man, you never let up!" He laid a bottle of dish soap on the sink counter.

"You expect me to wash myself with dish soap?"

"Works for dishes, it'll work for you."

"Are you going to stand there watching me?"

"What do you think I am, a peeping Tom?"

"How can I answer? I don't know you."

"And whose fault is that?" he asked, like a tutor questioning a recalcitrant student.

Shana sighed. "Mine."

Her captor gave her a thumbs up. "We're going on a field trip; your reward for all the behavioral reinforcement points you've accumulated."

Shana shuddered, but still needed to ask. "Where are we going?"

"We're off to find *Daddy Dearest*!"

Chapter 25

ALAN
MARCH 1983

Alan helplessly stood outside the bathroom door, listening to the *splat splat* pound the toilet bowl. Before slamming the door between then, his wife had fiercely warned him to Stay the Fuck Out!

This upchucking failed to signal morning sickness foretold no glimmer of hope; all this she'd bitterly assured him. Instead, her retching signified utter despair, grief.

"My babies are dead; I can't go on," she'd repeat like a mantra.

For the last four weeks, Deb had refused to accompany him to their therapy sessions. Therapy had been her idea. Now he was the one who was the therapist's insights like a lifeline while Deb slowly relinquished her rope.

In fact, the more cognizant and communicative he was with Deb over their shared loss, the more agitated she became. Dr. Gardner said his wife's exploding emotions were a healthy first step; a signal she felt safe enough with him to grieve, to mourn. Deep down inside, said the therapist, Deborah knew he would be present for her. That he'd cradle her as she sobbed, that he'd listen as she ranted against him for impregnating her with wimpy sperm.

The bathroom door flew open. His wife's tear-stained face mirrored his own.

"How can I help?" The psychologist had given him a list of open-ended questions which enabled parents who'd lost babies through miscarriage or death to reclaim some modicum of control over their lives. His assignment was to allow Deborah to make choices, no matter how minute. These choices would eventually enable her to reclaim a sense of control over her mind and body.

"How can you help?" she shrieked. "You can stop trying to be Mr. Perfect. You can stop treating me like some lab experiment. You can stop touching me like I'm broken!"

Alan recoiled. "But I thought that's what you wanted, what you needed, to heal!"

"When we saw Dr. Gardner, you opened up. You showed me your vulnerability, your insecurities, your fear that you'll never be able to give me a baby. That I'll leave you."

He cringed as that humiliating memory flashed before his eyes. "I opened myself up, not just to you, but a complete stranger. I confessed weaknesses. But it's never enough for you."

"That day, my love for you returned strong and true."

"So what's the problem?" he asked, perplexed.

"You stuck your head outside your shell. But then you quickly brought it back inside."

"I admitted I needed help. I began going to counseling and you quit!"

"Because I know what you do at those sessions."

"Yeah, talk…"

"…about deeply personal things you refuse to share when you and I are together."

Alan threw his hands in the air. "I'm going to the office."

"Go ahead, run away," she called after him.

He turned back to Deborah. "What do you want from me?"

"I need you to open your heart to me."

"That's what I've been doing," Alan protested.

"I'm not an exotic recipe to be figured out."

"You're the one still researching miscarriage and infant death," he accused.

"That was so we'd be on the same page. I want us to go through the five stages of grief together. We can't do that without a therapist's help."

Suddenly it all clicked. "You want us to go back to Dr. Gardner?"

Deb's face brightened. "It will strengthen our relationship."

Alan shuddered. He wasn't even familiar with the stages of grief on more than a superficial level. But building a fortress between him and his wife was not the answer. "I'm willing to give it a try, but no unrealistic expectations, agreed?"

"I'm not even sure I can meet my own expectations."

He grunted.

His wife's voice softened. "Alan?"

"Yeah?"

"I'm sorry for taunting you. I love you."

The relief he experienced was astounding. A glimmer of hope. That's all he'd been searching for. He took his wife in his arms. "Just don't let it happen again."

"Now your expectations *are* too high," she joked.

He broke away and punched the therapist's number into his phone.

Chapter 26

SHANA

The click of the ignition forced Shana from her so-called plan; the plan she'd not yet had time to devise. Lying prone, she watched as slivers of light floated throughout the Audi's vinyl interior. "Nothing like an early morning drive to nowhere," she mumbled.

"What?" One hand on the steering wheel, his eyes on the road, Daniel was futzing with the Sirius radio channels.

"I need to eat."

Meditation music wafted through the car. "You'll be the first to know when we stop."

"Seriously," she said. "I haven't eaten since breakfast yesterday."

"Actually, it was brunch but I won't quibble."

"So what's the plan?" she asked, desperately hoping Daniel had changed his mind.

"We're off to find Daddy Dearest, remember?"

Please, God, don't make me an accomplice, she prayed. "But he lives in Chicago."

"He made a business move to New York City nineteen years ago."

"I told you I don't know his name!"

"It's okay, I do."

Shana's arms were growing numb; she unsuccessfully attempted to raise her arms over her head. "How can you be sure you've got the right person?"

"Simple. I called Roosevelt University in Chicago, told them I was an alum, and ordered a copy of the yearbook from the year you graduated."

"That's bullshit," she said, relishing a zap of anger. "Roosevelt requires social security number, date of graduation, and current contact information before releasing that information."

He glared at her over his shoulder. "All you need to know is, I made it happen!"

"Oh, so now you're Superman?"

Her captor's voice turned sugary. "Chill. Nobody's going to do anything to you just yet."

Shana gasped.

"To show I'm a good guy, I'll let you in on a bit more about how I located Daddy Dearest." He leaned over the driver's seat again. "Sound good?"

She glared at him in response.

"I hacked into the student database from 1979 and borrowed a male student's personal information. Easy-peasy for a cybersecurity guy like me!"

He took pleasure in boasting about his accomplishments, Shana noted. Definitely her son. "You still haven't told me how you figured out his name."

"Can't give away all my trade secrets until we find Daddy."

"You've got his address?"

"Of course."

"You Googled all the people with the same name, age, and state of origin?"

"That was a wee bit tricky," he said humbly. "Took me days to narrow it down."

"My brilliant son. One more question."

Daniel slammed the steering wheel, then, like a re-take, touched it gently. "Yes?"

"Can you turn off the air conditioning? It's freezing back here.

Chapter 27

BECCA

Detective Hernandez stood at the foot of Rachel's hospital bed, delivering the crushing words: None of the 300 leads panned out. Her shocked expression was similar to that found in a slasher movie—a genre they both refused to watch.

"Twenty-thousand-dollars in reward money, three hundred leads, and nothing to show for it?" Rachel asked.

That question bounced off the walls as Daddy entered the room. He kissed Becca, and then made a beeline towards Rachel. "

How are you feeling, honey?" he asked, his voice fake cheerful. "Sorry I didn't visit last night, but I was emotionally and physically drained."

In the silence, Daddy noticed the detective's presence.

"Any update on my wife?" he asked, his voice hopeful.

The detective adopted a wide stance, laptop in hand. "Unfortunately, nothing yet."

Rachel's eyes were devoid of expression. "The reward money didn't work."

"I'm sorry to make you repeat yourself if you already told the girls, but can you summarize what you do and don't know at this juncture?"

Detective Hernandez leaned back, one foot pushing knee high against the wall. She scanned Mom's computer file. "We went back to the Boat House to interview the restaurant staff. Neither your waiter nor the hostess recall your wife returning to the restaurant."

That bitch who couldn't remember one purple-streaked haired woman, Becca thought.

"Neither the carriage drivers nor the mother wheeling a baby buggy recall seeing your wife after their initial interaction with her."

"You told them about the reward?" Rachel demanded.

Detective Hernandez nodded.

"What about joggers and families visiting Central Park Sunday afternoon?" Becca asked.

"The NYPD had thirty-one security cameras solely covering the park. It's a relatively safe site. Only sixty-five criminal acts reported per year, as opposed to thousands in Manhattan and the Bronx."

"What are you saying?" asked Rachel.

"The cameras caught your mother coming out of the restaurant, walking along the paved path, and then the wooded areas, and at the sites where the carriage drivers, as well as the water fountain where the woman with the baby were sighted. However, later in the day, a glitch in the Microsoft High Domain Awareness System occurred on three cameras. It's not certain if extremely high temperatures followed by a severe thunderstorm had a negative impact on the system."

"You're saying my wife could have been in the section of the Park where the malfunction occurred," Dad said softly.

Becca nibbled her fingernails. Mom could be in real danger.

"So what the hell are you doing about it?" asked Rachel.

Detective Hernandez leaned against the wall and stared at Rachel. "Why don't I shut up and let you tell me?"

Dad gives my sister a reproving look—a look both of us have only received a couple of times in our lives for serious acts, like underage drinking or copping candy at the grocery store. Then his eyes returned to the Detective. "Please, carry on."

"Before the software glitch occurred, your wife was videotaped lifting her arms to the sky and twirling during the rainstorm."

Becca's heart caught in her throat. Mom was all about expressing joy.

"The Park emptied of visitors. Then someone approached her."

Just then, Zander walked into the hospital room. Becca glanced at the wall clock. It was 5:15 p.m.

"Hey, Pa." He gave Dad a hug, nodded to me and the Detective, and kissed Rachel. Then he went to the sink to wash his hands. "Any word on Ma yet?"

"You're just in time to hear the latest," Becca said with false heartiness.

"Which is nothing," Rachel grumbled.

Detective Hernandez frowned. "My answer might have been misleading."

"Misleading, how?" Becca asked.

The detective's smile was almost imperceptible. No doubt, she was grateful Becca wasn't snarky like Rachel.

"This morning on NYPD Instagram, we received a picture of a woman stepping underneath an oversized black umbrella. That woman could be your mother."

"So you wait until now to tell us?" Rachel said.

Detective Hernandez's lips tightened.

Zan gave Rachel dirty look. He could tell she'd been giving the detective a hard time.

"Did the picture show who was holding the umbrella?" Becca asked.

"Unfortunately, not."

Dad went pale.

"However, at noon today we received a Pinterest photo of the first picture. Except this photo had been zoomed in. Although the umbrella completely covers the face, hands, and frontal view of the person, shoe prints are possible to make out."

"Spell it out for us, Detective," said Dad. "What do these findings indicate?"

"When we zoomed in on the shoe, itself, we noticed it was a high-top sneaker, brown rattlesnake print."

"Brand logo?" asked Zan.

"Don't need to know the logo," said Dad. It's a ConservaT.

Dad worked in a men's shoes wholesale liquidation business with their grandpa until 2018, when they both retired. He knew every brand of shoe there is.

"This is important why?" Rachel asked impatiently.

"Most people don't walk around in rattlesnake print gym shoes."

"So the person who kidnapped…"

"…last saw," Detective Hernandez interrupted.

"...my mother is the member of a gang?" asked Rachel.

Zan rolled his eyes. "No gang member's going to be taking a stroll through Central Park."

"You know all about gangs, huh?" said Rachel.

Zan threw his arms in the air. "You seriously have to work on your attitude unless you want to raise this baby with a chip on her shoulder!"

Becca wanted to second that statement, but she was scared of the blowout.

"Where did this lead come from?" asked Dad.

Detective Hernandez' voice took on a conciliatory note. "We're not sure yet, but we're working on it. We believe the person who sent the first picture and the person who sent the second picture are one and the same. However, the sender is using an alias."

"Well then, you better get going and find the guy in the snakeskin shoes who kidnapped our Mom!" Rachel said icily.

Zan shook his head, jumped to his feet, and stalked out the door.

"I was talking to the Detective," she shouted after him.

"He knows," Becca said wryly.

"We all do appreciate your hard work, Detective," said Daddy.

Becca glanced at Rachel. She shut her eyes and rubbed her tummy.

"Impressive!" joked Dad.

Nobody laughed.

"I'll be in touch," said Detective Hernandez as she exited the room.

Daddy excused himself to go to the bathroom down the hall.

Becca climbed into bed beside Rachel. "Sometimes you can be so obnoxious."

"I don't want to talk," she mumbled into her pillow.

"I'm scared, too, but you don't see me taking it out on the Detective, do you?"

"You're a better person than I am," she said drowsily.

"You shouldn't get so riled up. It's not good for the baby."

"I'm tired."

A memory marble hit Becca. It was December. Frigid cold. An electrical storm. Power outage. Telephone lines down. Daddy away on business. Dark skies. She and her sister freaking out. Mom lights candles. They all snuggled together beneath coats and blankets. Mom started singing an Israeli lullaby: "Tum ba la, tum ba la, tum ba la li la…."

As Rachel nestled her head in her pillow, Becca began to sing. "Tum ba la, tum ba la…."

Chapter 28

ALAN
APRIL 1983

Alan and Deborah sat together on the sofa facing Dr. Gardner. This session, Deb was talking non-stop.

"Alan and I went back to synagogue for the first time since our babies died."

Four months after the event, he still winced at the sound of the word.

"I'd read the newsletter wrong. Instead of the regular adult Shabbat service, it was the monthly parent-tot Shabbat service. Alan immediately wanted to slam out of the synagogue, but I thought I could make it through."

"She told me I could do whatever I want, but she was staying," Alan interrupted.

"The tot service only lasts an hour. I didn't want to be rude and leave."

Dr. Gardner looked at Alan. "How did that make you feel?"

"The truth?"

Dr. Gardner and Deborah both looked at him. He felt like an insect under a microscope. "Alone. I felt alone."

"What did 'alone' feel like?"

Alan stared at Deborah. "Like she didn't need me anymore. Like she could be strong all by herself. Like I was useless."

Silence permeated the office.

Finally Deborah spoke. "Your reactions are just your perception. Everything's about you."

"Thanks for that great insight," he retorted.

"What were the feelings behind your words when you told him he could leave but you were staying?" asked Dr. Gardner.

"I felt strong enough to endure watching all those little kids with their families."

"I wanted to protect you having to endure that painful experience," Alan said, exasperated.

Deborah took his hand and looked into his eyes. "I knew it would be painful, but I wanted to challenge myself."

"What happened then?" asked Dr. Gardner.

"I told her I'd pick her up later. Then I left."

"How did that make you feel, Deborah?"

"Part of me was furious that Alan deserted me, but another part of me was grateful; now I was free to react or not react to the experience without judgment."

"What did you discover about yourself?" asked Dr. Gardner.

Deborah swiped at her eyes. "I felt jealous that having healthy babies came so effortlessly to all these parents. The pain of watching mothers nurse their infants during services, when it had taken so long for my milk to dry up with nothing to show for it. The pain of listening to toddlers and their mommies and daddies sing the blessings and songs together. Try as I might, I couldn't stop my tears. But their joyful singing camouflaged my sobs! Allowing myself to express my rage felt cathartic. By the time Alan picked me up, I felt much calmer."

"She did seem less depressed," Alan confirmed.

"Depression is anger turned inward," said the psychiatrist.

Deborah smiled at him. "I threw my arms around Alan and thanked him for trusting me to go through that experience and not lose myself in the process."

He smiled back. "I was glad you weren't angry I left you alone at services. But I couldn't figure out why you were thanking me."

"What do you hear Deborah saying?" asked Dr. Gardner.

"That confronting, instead of denying, emotional pain helps a person heal."

Deborah hugged him. "I knew you were a compassionate person; it just took you awhile to show it."

"Thanks to Dr. Gardner's self-exploration homework," Alan said.

Dr. Gardner eyed her watch. "In our remaining minutes, I'd like to focus on you, Alan, if that's all right with both of you?"

Deborah shrugged. "Sure."

"That's cool," said Alan.

Dr. Gardner turned to Alan. "How has grief affected your professional life?"

Alan was struck dumb at the question. This was one thread he'd managed to conceal from the psychiatrist, although she'd broached it on more than one occasion. *Work makes the man,* as his father used to say. Alan preferred a more succinct saying: *Without work, man is a Loser.*

He glanced at his wife sitting beside him so expectantly. If not the psychiatrist, his wife deserved an answer. Breathing deeply, Alan chose to reveal his soul once again.

"A couple of weeks ago, one of my colleagues had a new baby. The office held a baby shower for her. I took one look at her and her baby—the pain was more than I could stand—put the gift on a table and ran out of the room.

"Later, she came to my office and asked if I was sick. 'Yeah, I'm sick at heart that you've given birth to a healthy, beautiful infant while God delivers dead babies to me and my wife'.

"Her jaw dropped. It was then I recalled she'd only recently started working here; no one had told her about my loss. I apologized over and over again for my rude remarks, but she closed her ears and fled my office.

"When did that happen?" asked Deborah.

"Last Friday."

A light of recognition touched her eyes. "The same evening as Tot Shabbat."

Alan nodded.

"So that's why you stomped out of temple when I told you to leave if you couldn't handle it."

He smiled thinly. "Bingo."

"How does that realization make you feel, Deborah?"

She placed a hand on her heart. "I'm grateful to begin to understand my husband better."

"And how did sharing this story make you feel, Alan?"

"I can't say it was a pleasant experience."

Both Deb and Dr. Gardner nodded.

"Sharing a story where I'm bad guy is painful. But I took a chance because I trust Deb to still love me afterwards."

"Why wouldn't I?" she asked, perplexed.

"A man should be strong, both physically and emotionally, but you're emotionally stronger than me."

"You went through the pain and came out the other side, same as I did," she said.

"How would you act differently if this kind of situation happens again at your workplace?" asked the therapist.

"Baby showers are not a common occurrence," said Alan.

"As more young people are recruited, there's bound to be more babies, right?" asked Deborah.

Alan racked his brain for a viable answer. None came to mind. He began to sweat.

"Do you need me to turn down the thermostat?" asked Dr. Gardner.

Alan shook his head.

"Are you feeling okay?" his wife asked anxiously.

This was a perfect storm. He could lie to them both; tell them he was feeling dizzy. They'd believe him. The only one he couldn't fool was himself. Damn, communicating was hard. Voicing ambivalence. Feeling stupid. Fearing reaction from others.

Free fall time. "I don't know if I would act differently in a similar situation."

"Something to discuss next session," said Dr. Gardner. "Are you planning to attend together from now on?"

Alan glanced at his wife. He'd taken a giant leap of trust and not fallen through the rabbit hole. Deb's face was glowing. Go figure. "Sure."

"Definitely," said Deb.

"You've both expressed your vulnerabilities today," said Dr. Gardner. "Before we end, can each of you share a few words about what you take from today's session?"

"Confiding challenges and asking for help grows a marriage," said Deb.

"Marriage means trusting your partner to accept your vulnerabilities, as well as your strengths," said Alan.

The psychiatrist stood and walked them into the office lobby. "Have a loving week."

"We will," Alan and Deborah said in unison.

Chapter 29

SHANA

Shana struggled against her captor as he re-shackled her wrists, tightened the rope around her ankles, and then dragged her fully clothed body into the backyard carport.

The sun was just beginning to peek through the sky as he laid her in the back seat of the silver Audi—she'd noticed its logo. Her feet were bare, and her toes had scraped the concrete driveway. Still, she emitted a croaky whistle. At least she'd go in style!

"Shut up! I need to think." Daniel slipped into the leather driver's seat and cupped his chin on the steering wheel.

Silence was Shana's Achilles' heel. Her favorite color was red. Her son had no idea that drama fed her soul. Not this kind of drama, of course! Then, again, she'd never have guessed a child of hers would grow up to be a kidnapper and, yes, a murderer. Daniel had said his grandmother died in a nursing home, but what if he was lying?

Today's excursion would brand Daniel accordingly. Shana couldn't allow him to kill his birth father. What good would she be to her husband and daughters if she broke free of her captor, after allowing him to commit such a horrific act? Either way, her son would kill her. Although Daniel hadn't said as much, Shana suspected he was only keeping her alive to witness The Deed.

This momentary silence would enable her to devise a plan, just as she did as a journalist when she elicited cold hard truths from white collar criminals. This time, both her life and that of her rapist were at stake.

Chapter 30

DEBORAH
MAY 1983

On her knees
Coyote Howling
    Clawing
        Begging
            Babies!

  Strangers
   Long coats
  Hats
  Eyes concealed

      Clutch babies
  Sink
  Into
Sheol

      On her knees
    Breasts overflowing
  Freezing on
Empty

No
Babies
Suckle

Agony

He
Chops.

    ON HER FEET
    SHRIEKING
    BEATING HIM

      JUMP

"No! No!"

Alan immediately awakened, clutched her to his chest. "You're okay. It was only a bad dream."

Deborah sobbed into his neck. "It was so real. Scary."

"Tell me."

"You axed the babies."

"Fortunately for you, my mommy taught me to never play with axes." he said, dark humor his forte. "What else?"

Deborah shivered. "We jumped into the babies' coffin—all the babies were buried in one vault—and the earth closed over us."

"Did we bring along a shovel?"

She pulled away from him. "How can you joke at a time like this?"

"A time like this is exactly when we need to laugh to keep from crying."

A ray of sunlight threatened to lighten Deborah's grief, but she didn't deserve quick relief. Instead, she imagined two of her babies coming through the birth canal, stillborn. Now she was in the appropriate state of mind.

"We need time to mourn. Dr. Gardner said so."

"We've been doing that for the last five months. How much longer do we immerse ourselves in this pain before we crack?"

Deborah's breath was coming in short spurts. "Our mourning is going to last forever. It said so in my dream."

"That idea was nowhere in your dream."

"The part about you and I falling into the babies' grave and the earth covering us up? It's like when God ordered the earth to swallow Aaron's sons for not trusting in the Lord. It means God is going to strike us dead for killing our children."

"God has already killed us, don't you think?"

"God will kill us for not trusting Him to bless us with a child of our own."

Alan looked at her, flummoxed. "Those three babies you delivered were our own."

"No, Alan. A sperm donor impregnated me. I committed adultery."

"For God's sake, Deb."

She interrupted him. "Do not take God's name in vain."

"His sperm and your eggs came together in a petri dish! I'm worried about you. You seemed better since you started going to Dr. Gardner, but now it's like you're regressing."

"Two steps forward. One step back. That's what Dr. Gardner said. If you can't handle that, you should leave."

Alan stared at her. "What?"

"I'll give you a quickie divorce. Whether or not it will be Kosher doesn't matter. You don't believe in God anymore, anyway."

"I never said that!"

"Find a nice Jewish girl with no baggage; someone who doesn't want children, because your plumbing is definitely out of order."

Alan winced. "That was so below the belt."

It felt like someone had snuck into her brain, confiscated her words, and twisted them into putty. Deborah was helpless to do anything but egg him on. "Maybe I'm no longer *your* Deb. Did you ever think of that?"

Alan stood and backed away from the bed. "You're overwrought. You need to rest."

She waved him away. "Get out and don't come back!"

Chapter 31

DETECTIVE HERNANDEZ

Detective Hernandez placed the Shana Kahn file on her desk. Then she glanced at the husband and younger daughter sitting across from her. "We've come up with a solid lead."

David Kahn sat forward. "What did you find out?"

"One of the park security cameras indicates a man began following your wife soon after she left the restaurant. We showed his picture to the vendors and got a hit; the frozen ice vendor served him just as the thunderstorm began. The man bid him salaam and fled the park."

"That means peace in Arabic," said Becca Kahn, the younger daughter.

Hernandez set the photo before them. "Do you recognize this man?"

Kahn brought the picture to eye level. "He looks familiar."

"Can I see?"

Kahn handed the picture to his daughter.

She held it up close.

Hernandez noted the widening of the girl's pupils, quickly masked. "Not sure."

"Is it possible the camera videotaped a park visitor who merely happened to be walking behind my wife?" asked Kahn.

"The suspect followed your wife into the woods, then back onto the paved path."

Hernandez noticed the father and daughter exchange a worried glance.

"If you know this man's identity, you need to tell me."

"So you think this man is a suspect because of his walking path and frozen ice purchase?" asked Kahn.

"Did he even have a golf umbrella?" the younger daughter broke in.

"The frozen ice vendor recalls he was wearing a black hat, but no umbrella."

"I'm thinking it's unlikely this man kidnapped my wife."

Detective gave him a cynical look. "What I'm thinking, Mr. Kahn, is that you and your family staged this whole missing persons thing for publicity."

"That's ridiculous," he sputtered. "We don't even live in New York."

"Maybe you paid someone to get rid of your wife."

"This is ludicrous! I love my wife. I want you to find her."

"Really, because it looks like neither you nor your daughter care about getting her back."

The girl's cheeks reddened. "Dad and I don't want to accuse anybody of anything unless we're sure."

Kahn gave his daughter a sharp look.

"That's for us to determine, not you," Hernandez chastised her.

The girl ignored her father's warning. "We'll let you know by tonight if the man in the picture is the person we think he is."

"Or I could hold you and your dad in jail until you come clean."

"Do I need to hire an attorney?" asked Kahn, his voice strong and steady.

"Please," the girl pleaded. "Just give us a few hours and we'll give you an answer."

Detective Hernandez shrugged. "Every additional minute a person remains missing increases the odds of a negative outcome. But it's your family member, not mine." She checked the wall clock. "You've got until 7 p.m. to contact me. If I don't hear from you, I'm going to arrest you for concealing evidence of a crime."

"Thank you, detective," said Kahn, rising to his feet. "We just want to be sure."

Detective Hernandez shooed father and daughter out of her office. "Hange 7 p.m. to 7:00 p.m."

CHAPTER 32

ALAN
JUNE 1983

The morning after their fight, Deborah had called him at the *Holiday In*n to apologize. "I'm not taking back my feelings, only the nutso way I expressed them."

Alan almost told his wife he needed a couple more days to process what happened; instead, here he was, back at home, unpacking his toothbrush and pajamas.

He still didn't understand where he'd gone wrong. He'd followed the psychiatrist's suggestions; been more solicitous of his wife's feelings, looked her in the eye when she spoke to him, let her help decide what movie or television program to watch, cuddled without demanding sex, and even cooked dinner a couple of times a week. Sure, he'd made a couple of mistakes along the way. He never said he was perfect.

How could he tell her he strained at the leash to flee his pain while she insisted on working through hers by staying in the moment? His inability to "man up," coupled with his inability to produce healthy offspring, confirmed he was a wuss.

Maybe he should have taken the hint when Deb told him to get out. Maybe the kindest thing for him to do was

Her dad looked at her like she had tree branches growing from her head.

"Rachel's going to think something's wrong if we show up twice in one day."

"There is something wrong!" Becca loved her dad, but confrontation was his Achilles heel.

"You can't talk to your sister about this."

"Would you rather I talk to Zan or his mom instead?"

Dad's face dropped.

"Sorry, Daddy." The girls usually saved their shouting for mom's ears only.

"This news could make her go into labor. Wait until after she has the baby."

Becca went silent. The last thing she wanted was for her words to force her sister into premature delivery. How many times in the past had they slammed their mother over using poor timing to deliver bad news?

Becca considered what her mother would say if she was there, now.

"At the end of the day, we each have to live with the decisions we make. Do what lightens your soul."

What would lighten her soul would be to tell Rachel the truth; her husband's stepdad may have kidnapped their mom. Not that she believed that the guy who lifted her from the ground when she'd fallen could have done something that awful. But bad guys aren't bad 24/7; they work, eat, pee, and watch TV just like the rest of us.

In that same way, good people are not good, day in, day out. There'd been lots of times when she and Rachel had hurt mom's feelings so badly, she cried. Other times, they were all lovey-dovey. They played games together, went on mini-vacations, made each other laugh, and listened to each other's problems. Mom even told them her problems—sometimes TMI—because she didn't want to worry their dad, and the only friends she had were from work.

The cab driver stopped his meter.

"Thirty dollars," he said in a heavily accented voice.

Becca and her dad both reached for their wallets, but she won. "Here you go."

When he saw her generous tip, the driver smiled through the rear view mirror. She gave him a thumbs up.

She needed to give herself that same gesture for whatever would come next.

Chapter 34

ALAN
DECEMBER 1983

Alan and his wife sat side by side, holding hands. "It's unreal this is our final therapy session with you."

Dr. Gardner leaned back in her swivel chair. "How does that make you feel?"

"Like a ship that's lost its anchor," he said.

Deborah gently removed her hand from his. "Like a rainbow that's lost its colors."

"It's like that old Neil Sedaka song," said Alan. "*Breaking Up is Hard To Do.*"

Deb stared at the psychiatrist. "What are we going to do without your guidance? My family still isn't speaking to us, and Alan's father's got dementia."

"He's been off his rocker for a long time, now," said Alan.

Deb glanced at him. "More so since the babies died."

"You mentioned in the past that your mother passed away a couple of years ago."

Alan nodded.

"Both you and Deborah are survivors. You've weathered this storm all by yourselves, with no family support."

"My brother's still talking to me. The temple members and the rabbi have been very supportive."

"The second support group you sent us to was really helpful, even though I had to drag this guy there, kicking and screaming," teased Deborah.

Alan smirked.

"Now you just have to work on sharing your feelings with me," she said.

"Hey, I am getting better."

Deborah rolled her eyes. "Slowly. Very slowly."

Alan detected an edge to her words. "When we married, I never promised to be perfect."

His wife kissed him on the cheek. "I promised to take you for better or for worse."

"So I was 'for worse'?"

"For a few months, there, yeah."

Alan turned toward his wife. "Fully reentering life after the babies died has been damn hard for me, too."

"I know," Deborah said, her voice soothing.

"Know the feelings of loss and mourning you both experienced this year will probably come up during Chanukah services, when you watch little kids light their menorahs at temple. You'll feel it again at Purim, when the kids dress in costumes. You'll especially feel it at Passover, when you get to the section in the Haggadah that mentions the Four Sons."

They exchanged panicked expressions.

"I bring this subject up, not to make you feel worse, but to encourage you to discuss whether or not to attend

Chanukah and Purim services. Rabbi Shapiro would understand."

"You want us to discuss this now?" asked Alan.

"She means we discuss it when we get home, honey."

"But tomorrow's the first night of Chanukah."

"We'll discuss it when we get home," Deborah repeated.

Alan shrugged. "Whatever."

Dr. Gardner glanced at her watch. "Before our session ends, I want to provide clarification. Although your feelings of loss will remain intense for a while, they will eventually dissipate. You will have flashbacks of the event and cry unexpectedly, you will still experience the occasional nightmare. But you will get through those feelings together. I am always here for you both. Don't hesitate to phone and set up an appointment."

Deborah rose to give the psychiatrist a hug. "We couldn't have done it without you."

Alan followed suit. "Absolutely. Thank you for all your help."

"Keep communicating with each other. You both possess the tools now. God Bless."

As Alan and his wife left the office, he muttered. "If life gets too tough, we can always commit *Hari Kari*."

Deborah pulled his face eye-level to hers. "No talk of suicide, understand? We need to stay alive to honor our children's memory. Promise."

He would try. He would really try.

Chapter 35

BECCA

Becca and her dad *whooshed* into the hospital room—she was the only one to whoosh; dad navigated his cane across the threshold. A green curtain separated them from Rachel's bed.

"Hey," Becca called.

Zan stepped out from behind the curtain. "Hey Pa, Bec."

Becca's heart quickened. "Is Rach okay?"

"The doctor's examining her," he said.

"Just get here?" asked dad.

"Yeah, Rachel texted me, so I left work a few minutes early."

"She misses you," joked daddy.

Zan glanced back at the curtain before he responds. "Not so much."

The vibes in the room felt all wrong.

"What's going on?" Becca asked.

"After they wheeled Rachel back from Ultrasound, she had a small amount of vaginal bleeding. The doctor's checking to make sure the baby's okay."

"She'll be fine," Daddy said in a reassuring voice.

As if on cue, the green curtain opens a quarter-way and Doctor Nayman stepped toward them. She frowned.

Becca's body tensed. "How are my sister and the baby doing?"

"Fortunately, we were able to stop Rachel's bleeding; the minimal amount she lost doesn't seem to have adversely impacted the baby. For now, we'll be keeping a close watch on both of them."

"Thank God," said Dad.

Zan excused himself to go sit by Rachel.

"I do need to caution you about concerning one issue," said the doctor.

Dad and Becca regard each other. They both know what that issue was.

The doctor confirmed their prediction.

"Rachel is quite agitated over your wife's disappearance. Stress is dangerous for her and the baby. If your daughter goes into labor at this point in her pregnancy, chances are your grandchild could be born with underdeveloped brain, lungs, sight, and hearing. I'm sure this is not the outcome your family is hoping for."

"Of course, I want my grandchild to be delivered full or near full-term for all the reasons you mentioned. But Rachel is a stubborn young woman. Once she takes it into her head to obsess about her mother's disappearance, she won't be distracted."

The doctor's silence suggested she was not pleased with dad's response.

"We'll do all we can to reduce my sister's stress," Becca said. "Rachel meditates and does deep breathing exercises, and we've got positive news about mom, which should make her feel better."

Now the doctor was all smiles. "We're all praying for your mother's safe return."

"Thank you for your encouragement," said dad.

The doctor placed her palms together. "Many blessings." Then she pulled back the curtain.

Becca softly greeted her sister.

"How you feeling, Old Yeller?"

Rach's eyes fluttered open and she gave her a weak smile. "Fine, Lassie." Her voice sounded groggy.

Dr. Nayman pulled Zan aside, but her words echoed. "Make sure your wife uses the bedside chamber pot. She needs to remain in bed for 24 hours."

Becca noted the old-fashioned words, wondering what country the doc was from.

"Promise," said Zander.

The doctor left the room.

Daddy turned his attention to Rachel. "You've had a long day. Take a nice rest. We'll all be here when you get up."

Rach began to toss and turn. "Where's Mommy? Why isn't she here?"

Zander smoothed her hair. "Sh. It's all gonna be okay, babe."

Her voice rose a decibel. "I need mom!"

She sounded delirious. Becca pressed the nurse's button.

The nurse hurried into the room and eyed Rachel's blood pressure chart.

Rachel shook her head from side to side. "Mommy? Where are you?"

"You need to calm down, sweetie," said the nurse as she cuffed her arm. At the sight of the results, she rushed from the room. Moments later, she returned with an oxygen mask which she placed over Rachel's nose and mouth.

"Breathe in, breathe out." Rachel did as she was told.

The nurse hooked Rachel up to an IV bag and attached it to the pole. She wasn't going to appreciate dragging the pole around with her again, but she had to stay in bed, anyway.

"This should relax you," the nurse told her.

Within seconds, Rachel's body had stopped twitching. Soon she was snoring away.

The nurse exited the room.

Becca and her dad took their seats, but Zan continued to smooth Rach's hair.

"I put up with my wife's snoring every night," he whispered.

"Tell me about it. I've had to put up with my wife's snoring for forty years!"

"I don't snore," Becca said proudly.

"You get the Non-Snoring Golden Matzo Ball Award!" Dad said.

"Thank you," she said, panning for a selfie.

A dinner cart arrived with Rachel's food. Zan moved the cart away from the bed. "Rach mentioned you guys visited earlier today. What brings you back a second time?"

Shoot! Her brother-in-law wasn't supposed to be present for true confessions.

Becca glanced at her dad. He gave her a look that said *don't even think about it.*

Zan looked from dad to her and back again.

"Bet you guys are starving. Cafeteria's open 'til six. How 'bout I run downstairs and get you both some food?"

Becca snickered.

He looked at her quizzically.

"We went through this same scenario at lunch, only with dad, me, and Rach," she explained.

He grinned. "Be right back, then."

If Zan left now, Becca knew she wouldon't have the courage to bring the topic up later, so she plunged ahead. "Before you go, your question deserves an answer."

He looked at her. "Okay. What's up?"

Becca balled her fists beneath her thighs. "Detective Hernandez received a valid lead about mom's disappearance."

"Terrific. Who is it?"

"Somebody our family might know."

"Really? Did she give you guys a name?"

Becca shook her head. "She showed us a couple of pics."

"Got them with you?" Zan asked.

"It's late," said dad. "Let's do this tomorrow."

Her dad was trying to warn her off, but it was time for her to lighten her soul.

Becca reached into her purse for the security camera pictures.

Chapter 36

DEBORAH
FEBRUARY 1984

Alan would be home from work any minute now. Tonight was Purim, and Deborah had just finished preparing the festive meal commemorating the salvation of the Jews through the leadership of Queen Esther. She smiled to herself as she carved the brisket in thin slices, just the way her husband liked it. She spooned homemade mashed potatoes and broccoli into the china serving bowls her mother had given her for a wedding present. She poured kosher grape wine into crystal glasses and placed them at their place settings, along with dinner plates, cutlery, and napkins. Life was easy when everything and everybody had an assigned place to be, to go.

In preparation for tonight's dinner, Deborah had pumped herself up with antidepressants, increasing her dosage from 20 mg to 50 mg. She'd recently begun to see Dr. Gardner again, this time for individual therapy. At last week's appointment, the psychiatrist had cautioned her to only raise the dosage level by 5 mg at a time to see how her body reacted. But tonight was a special night for more than one reason. Deborah couldn't allow her continued grief overshadow the special gift God had bestowed upon her earlier today.

Last month, at the one-year anniversary of their death, time had stopped for both her and Alan. They'd taken a nosedive. The rabbi had come to pray with them and wish them God's blessings for the future. But they'd buried themselves in a vault of memories and lacked enough energy to claw their way out.

However, therapy and anti-depression medicine had snatched her from the dungeon; given her hope that maybe she could birth a healthy baby in the future. When Alan noticed her positive change in attitude, he'd also resumed therapy and medication.

Bit by bit, communication between her and Alan improved. Happiness shimmered in their hearts. Then Purim had come along and shoved reality in their faces.

It was devastating to realize this would have been the babies' first Purim. She and Alan would have dressed their three babies in teeny tiny Mordecai shirts.

They would have sounded the grogger to blot out wicked Haman's name—but not loud enough to scare the babies.

They'd have given each baby a drop of wine from their pinkie fingers. They'd have settled the babies in a stroller for triplets and wheeled them down the street to Synagogue for the Megillah reading about how Queen Esther saved the Jewish people from the wicked Haman.

On the first day of Purim, she and Alan would have put their babies in their stroller and gone door to door, delivering Purim baskets filled with nuts, chocolate, candies, and baked goods to their Jewish neighbors. When they returned home, they'd have taken their babies' tiny fingers and helped them place silver coins in a Tzedakah box to feed the poor.

All these blessings, God had snatched from her and Alan. But this morning's unexpected phone call had enabled her to see the light, and she was upping her anti-depression meds to ensure nothing interfered when she shared the news with her husband.

Chapter 37

BECCA

"Don't do this, Becca," her dad whispered.

"If this is a bad time," said Zander, "I can look at the pics tomorrow."

The truth must come out. It felt like she'd been sitting in the dental chair, waiting for her wisdom teeth to be extracted. This time, she was the one doing the extracting. Her voice trembled as she pulled the pictures from her purse. "Now is fine."

"No!" Her dad's lips form the word, but it was too late.

Becca handed the pictures to her brother-in-law. She prepared for the worst. Neither he nor her sister would ever talk to her again. They'd accuse her of betraying them. Toss her in the nearest dumpster. Wipe their hands of her. Vomit filled her mouth. She rushed to the bathroom.

Before she could shut the door, she hears Zan's voice. "These pics are smeared, Bec. Your water bottle must be leaking."

Saved! Her nausea disappeared.

Dad breathed a sigh of relief.

"Maybe I can recognize the guy if you describe him," Zan said helpfully.

"Let's revisit this discussion tomorrow," Dad said firmly.

Seriously, Becca wanted nothing more than to put this *stepdad as suspect* thing to bed. Mom used that term when a newspaper edition was ready to be printed. If they didn't find her soon, she was going to die of grief.

But if she and her dad weren't back in Detective Hernandez's office by 7 p.m., the police would be coming for their family—at least Zan's family. She walked over to her brother-in-law.

"Do not tempt fate a second time," Dad murmured.

She breathed in deeply. Then she spoke. "The guy they found looks like John Belushi. Black sunglasses. Black hat. Black suit. Black shoes. On the chubby side."

Zander adopted *The Thinker* pose. "Age?"

She glanced at Dad. He was shaking his head in disgust.

"Forty-something."

"Hm. Doesn't sound like anyone I know. I can ask Mom or Kaiden, though."

Shoot! Zander's younger brother would be dragged into the investigation. Oh, how she wanted to let her dad convince her that everything was going to be fine. But there was no way she could deny the aardvark in the room. If Zan's stepdad was involved in her Mom's disappearance, she needed to follow through, no matter the consequences.

"Maybe the guy is a blues entertainer at a restaurant," Zan says.

Becca set fire to caution. "Maybe the guy is Aamer."

"My step-father?" He sounded incredulous.

She nodded.

Dad placed his head in his hands. "Aamer might be the last person to see my wife alive."

"That's crazy. Your mom doesn't even know my step-dad."

"Actually she does. They had a long chat on the restaurant patio before our name was called."

"Okay, so they talked. What's the connection to Ma's disappearance?"

Dad spoke slowly. "Evidently, their chat wasn't so friendly."

"Meaning?"

Becca cleared her throat. "My mom interviewed your step-dad about the Koran."

"Did he get angry?"

"He told her he'd happily answer all her questions."

"Did she ask him anything else?"

"Mom asked about the relationship between ISIS and the Koran. Afterward, I really laid into her about being so rude."

"Ma gets a little out there sometimes, but this doesn't sound like one of those times. Aamer is Muslim. He probably enjoyed teaching her about his religion."

"Then why did he sit at the opposite end of the brunch table from us? And why did he disappear after Mom left the restaurant?"

"Nothing to do with Ma. Aamer drives a flower truck on the weekends."

"So your mother said, but that doesn't make sense when he could make big bucks taxiing on the weekends instead, right?"

"How would I know? I haven't spoken to my mother's second husband for a decade!"

The resentment in his voice made Becca take a step back.

"I still don't understand the problem." Zan's voice rose.

"Is everything okay?"

Rachel's groggy voice echoed through the hospital room.

Chapter 38

DEBORAH
FEBRUARY 24, 1984

Deborah pulled her husband to her and planted a big juicy kiss on his lips. "How was your day at work?" He pulled back to stare at her. Usually all he got was a peck on the cheek. As he returned her ardent kiss, she knew new beginnings were at hand.

When they came up for air, she watched Alan eye the linen tablecloth and china dishes. "Is tonight a special occasion, or have you finally recognized what a great catch I am?"

Deborah beamed. "Definitely the latter."

She followed him to the guest bathroom as he washed his hands. "Actually, tonight is Erev Purim."

He dried his hands on a hand towel. "Totally slipped my mind. What time do we need to be at the Megillah reading?"

She led him back into the dining room and plopped a yarmulke on his head. "Let me worry about that. All you need to do right now is enjoy the fabulous meal I made you."

Alan took a seat. "The beef brisket and carrot tzimmes look delicious, and you drenched the mashed potatoes in margarine, just the way I like it."

It was a shame her husband couldn't smell the full-bodied scent of onions and garlic. Even the mouth-watering smell of cooked carrots, honey, and prunes—the recipe her mom had made her and her sister when they were young—would forever escape his notice. But tonight, she refused to dwell on Alan's reoccurring sinus infections, or anything else that would destroy the positive vibe they had going on.

Deborah felt guilty about not cooking for him as she should. In the year since the babies' passing, she'd been too depressed to prepare more than the bare minimum for holiday and Shabbat celebrations.

She recited the blessing over the holiday candles. Then she joined her husband in saying the blessings over the wine and challah. As she was about to dive into her food—she hadn't eaten all day in anticipation of sharing this morning's news—Alan asked: "No matzo ball soup?"

Deborah squelched her feeling of annoyance and answered brightly. "I didn't want us to be late for synagogue."

"That's cool," he said, digging into his food.

When they'd almost cleaned their plates, Deborah threw out the gauntlet. "My mom called this morning."

Alan raised his fork midair. "Why?"

"She apologized for separating us from family all these months when we needed them."

He put his fork down and stared at her. "What did you say?"

"I told her I forgive her."

"No way! Your mother can't expect us to pretend like nothing's happened! Like we're just one big happy family!"

Deborah reached across the table to touch his arm. "It is not for us to judge one another."

"Don't give me that shit! What kind of mother cuts herself off from her daughter and son-in-law because she disagrees with a decision they made—a gut-wrenching decision at that?"

"She didn't know it would hurt us so badly."

Alan threw his crumpled napkin on the table and jumped to his feet. "I'm not into games. Accept your mother back into your life, if you want, but don't expect me to do the same."

Deborah's heart quickened, despite the increased dosage of antidepressants she'd taken just a few hours ago. "Forget the dishes. I'll meet you in the car."

"Suddenly I'm not feeling celebratory anymore. Go yourself."

Her husband stalked from the room.

Chapter 39

SHANA

"As my grandmother used to say, 'You don't like it, take your business to Walgreens.'"

Her captor's joke was unexpected; better that response than pummeling her. Switching gears on her captor was also a distraction from locating, then executing, his birth father. "It really is freezing back here. I also have to pee."

Shana knew she was walking a fine line regarding Daniel's mood changes; for sure, he was bi-polar like her own grandfather. Where the hell were the police? Had her family even reported her missing?

She began to hyperventilate.

"I reset the air, but bathroom break won't be for another thirty minutes, so hang tight."

Her throat was so dry. Shana was finding it difficult to swallow. Had he been lying about his grandma's house being located near Central Park, she wondered? What if he'd drugged her at the park that first day, and then driven her to a neighboring state? She'd never been to New York before. Except for the Statue of Liberty and Times Square, she had no knowledge of landmarks.

"Ugh!" Visions of her husband, her daughters, her unborn grandchild, flit through her consciousness. *All you need is love, darlin,*' shouted her mother's voice from beyond.

Just then, she felt the car swerve, then come to an abrupt stop, causing her roped body to fall to the carpet. "Now what?" said her captor as he yanked open her car door.

His expression immediately turned to alarm. Shana struggled to follow his movement as he withdrew a thin vial from the glove compartment. "Stay with me. You're going to be okay."

As her throat began to close, she dizzily wondered whether her captor was asking her to remain with him rather than return to her family, or if his words had a different meaning.

She was beginning to lose consciousness when she suddenly felt a pin prick her arm.

Shana's eyes flew open. Attempted to swallow. Swallowed! Attempted to breathe. Breathed! "You saved my life! It's a miracle!"

Her captor carefully wrapped the vial in a clean tissue. "Now I know who I inherited my panic disorder from."

"But I don't have…"

"Figured you'd deny it."

Although she'd had a couple of anxiety meltdowns over the last couple of years, this experience had been way different. No use trying to convince Daniel he was mistaken. Instead, she thanked God for keeping her alive. Maybe she'd even start going to temple after a twenty-six-year sabbatical.

"That was Chlordiazepoxide, by the way."

"What?" His words brought her out of her reverie.

"Librium."

Shana gasped. Maybe her son was a doctor, every Jewish mother's dream. Then again, maybe he was selling opiate drugs.

Immediately, Daniel was by her side. "Feeling sick again?"

"Are you a drug pusher?" she asked through gritted teeth.

Her captor guffawed. "I told you, I work for DCFS."

"But it's against the law to…"

"…carry narcotics. I get a panic attack every three to four months, and deep breathing exercises and yoga only take me so far."

"You actually did inherit my panic attacks from my DNA," Shana admitted. Her first attack had occurred decades ago; the first time she'd been taken hostage. She pushed that image from her mind.

Daniel closed the front passenger door. "Now, that wasn't so hard to admit, was it?"

"Do you see a therapist?"

"I've done DBT therapy, which deals with post-traumatic stress, but it didn't work for me."

Shana's heartbeat dropped an octave at the dual revelations: Not only had her son experienced PTSD, he'd undergone a specific therapy most often used with those in the penal system. "You've been in prison?"

"What do you think?"

Not trusting Daniel's positive mood change, Shana replied with caution. "I'd say yes," Several years ago, she'd written a story on six incarcerated male adolescents who'd been arrested for violent crimes. After undergoing dialectical behavior therapy, they'd been better able to reflect on their actions, advocate for themselves, control their emotional outbursts, and tolerate stress without going off the deep end.

"Doesn't matter. There's no hope for me, either way, which is why I don't care if I get convicted for kidnapping you or for copping anti-anxiety drugs on the black market—or for any other nefarious act I perform in the future."

Once a reporter, always a reporter; wasn't that what her daughters complained about? Although her current dilemma was personal, Shana knew they'd agree her questions were necessary. "How did you get hold of an SSRI drug? Did you attempt to get a doctor's prescription for the SSRI vaccine?"

Daniel's face reddened. He clenched his fists. "I offer you closure on the man who raped you, and all you've got is more questions?"

"I didn't ask for clo…."

"Enough." He grabbed her body from the floor of the Audi's black interior. Then he tossed her over his shoulder like a tapestry carpet and began hiking down a gravel road.

"Where are you taking me?" Shana asked fearfully.

"My most recent adoptive mother was high maintenance. I don't need another one."

The wooded path did not look promising. "Wait! No more questions. Just bring me back to the car."

Now he was jogging, her chin bopping against his shoulders. "You said you don't need closure. That's fine by me. I already have birth daddy's address and zip code."

"Untie me!"

They came to a secluded area by a lake. "You need to be taught a lesson."

He carefully laid her body on the shore flanking the water. "Just a heads up, Google says these woods are home to foxes and bears."

"There's no wild animals an hour out of Manhattan," she retorted.

"Of course, you know it all. I'll be back for you tonight, if a two-legged or four-legged animal doesn't get you first." He turned and started to trek back in the direction they'd come.

"Daniel!" Shana shrieked after him. "Don't leave me here like this, without water, food or a way to defend myself!"

"Why did you save me from dying, then?"

"Nobody dies from a panic attack."

"And my bladder infection?"

Throwing his arms in the air, her son disappeared from sight.

Facts tumbling through her mind, like clothes in the dryer, Shana attempted to put the pieces together. If Daniel was telling the truth about purchasing narcotics solely for himself on the black market, and if, as she guessed, Daniel had committed an assortment of misdemeanors before age eighteen, resulting in DBT therapy, and if, as she also suspected, he was bi-polar, her son was on a one-way ticket to—she remembered the television documentary—Riker's Island. Add kidnapping and murder to the mix, and there would be no return.

Her son's fate, and possibly her own, were sealed, and there was nothing she could do about it.

CHAPTER 40

RACHEL

Rachel gazed warily at the family members gathered at the foot of her bed. "You guys already visited today. Is everything okay?"

"We were in the neighborhood and thought we'd drop by," said Dad.

"You are such a bad liar!"

Her dad looked chastened.

"Seriously, what's going on?"

"You were getting contractions and Pa and Bec were worried about you," said Zander.

Rachel let out a relieved breath. "Aw. I am so lucky to have such a caring family. Did you guys eat dinner yet?"

"Meantime, you can look at the pictures your sister brought."

"Cafeteria closes in fifteen minutes," said Zan."

Rachel glanced at the wall clock above the mounted T.V. "Better hurry."

"OMG. You found more pics of grandpa and grandma?"

"The detective gave Bec and your dad a couple of pics of a guy she thinks we might recognize."

Rachel extended her hand. "Let's see! Maybe he's a link to finding Mom."

Her sister hesitated, then handed her the smeared pics. Rachel squinted at the poor-quality copies. "Hmm. All I see is a chubby guy in a black jacket and hat. It's really hard to make out his facial features."

Zan took the pages from her hands. "That's what I said. But Bec says the detective texted her copies of the original photos."

She frowned at her sister. "So why are we looking at poor facsimiles when you've got the real thing?"

"I couldn't find the originals at first," Becca hedged.

"You got them now?"

"We probably should get our food first, then look at the pics later," said Dad.

"What's the big deal?"

Becca was quiet.

"Let's see the pictures!" Rachel demanded.

Her sister sighed as she handed her a sealed white business envelope. "Here you go."

Then she hurried from the hospital room.

◇◇◇◇◇◇◇◇◇

Rachel handed the two pictures to her husband. "I've only met your step-dad once, but this kind of looks like him. Wasn't he wearing those clothes and hat at brunch on Sunday?"

Zan gazed at the pictures, his eyebrows furrowed. "I agree with all of you. This is definitely Aamer. The detective gave Becca these pictures to show us because…"

"…she thinks he's a possible suspect in my mom's disappearance," interrupted Rachel.

"Or a witness," Zan added.

Dad cleared his throat. "Park surveillance cameras showed your step-dad in close proximity to Shana after she left the restaurant."

Rachel stared at her husband. "That's impossible. Your mom told us Aamer left the restaurant early because he had a flower delivery."

"Surveillance videos look convincing, even to an uneducated observer like me," said Dad.

Zan paced the hospital room. "What else did the cameras show?"

"The first video showed your step-dad stopping at a frozen ice vendor my wife had just passed. In another video he was couple hundred feet behind when she made it to Belvidere Castle. The last video caught him watching from the distance as Shana conversed with a horse & carriage driver."

Zan stopped pacing. "Does my mom know about these videos?"

"Not to my knowledge," Dad said.

"Let's keep it that way until we know for sure," said Zan.

"We're going to know very soon, in fact," said Dad.

"How?" asked Rachel.

Her sister breezed through the door, pocketing her cell phone. "Because Detective Hernandez is bringing Aamer down to the police station for questioning, as we speak."

Chapter 41

ALAN
APRIL 1984

His fists clenched beneath the dining room table, Alan restrained himself from bolting from the seder table as his niece and nephew sang the Four Questions from the Passover Haggadah. His babies would never lift their tiny voices to ask those questions, nor hear the story of their ancestors' exodus from Egypt. His babies were in the grave. His babies would never lift their tiny voices to ask those questions. His babies were in the grave.

Deborah's mother and sister were kvelling, their smiles reaching the tips of their foreheads. Alan looked across the table at his wife. She solemnly returned his gaze, reflecting their mutual pain. Her face was pale, her eyes dull blue, like she'd just recovered from a fatal illness, which, in a manner of speaking, she had.

A certain irony connected fatal illness with dead babies: upon initially receiving the sorrowful news, well-wishers were plentiful. They brought enough dinners to fill a utility freezer. They showered the family with offers to run errands. They visited so often that privacy seemed a distant dream.

Soon the grieving family began to take this attention for granted. *We're fine, really! We'll give you a call, get together when things settle down.* Except there was no *settling down*. There never would be *settling down*.

Their blithe words didn't fool anybody; not friends, not family, not work colleagues. They got the message.

They were not wanted. Their calls and visits tapered, until the grievers were left to face each other, day after day, night after night. A living hell.

Want to split? Alan mouthed.

The shake of Deb's head was almost imperceptible.

You sure? He asked with his eyes.

She gave him the tiniest of smiles.

In the Passover Haggadah, they'd come to the section: *The Four Children.* Four participants at the table respectively asked one question from the perspective of a wise child, a wicked child, a simple child, or the child who doesn't know enough to ask a question. Alan noticed that unlike in past years, Deborah's mother Libby was picking people at random to read. Please, God, I promise to go to minion every morning if her mom passes over my name.

God must have been attending another seder, because, his mother-in-law's tinny voice rose from the opposite end of the twelve-foot table. "Alan, can you please read the next child?"

Flustered, he said, "I lost my place. Which son is it?"

"The child who doesn't know enough to ask a question," Leah, Deb's sister, said, her voice artificially bright.

Alan looked at Deb. This last question was his least favorite. He cleared his throat. "Could you possibly choose someone else to read this one, and I can read another?"

Leah shot daggers with her eyes. "That's the only question left. It would be great to get through this seder soon so the kids can eat."

Her mother turned to Leah. "Why don't you read this question yourself, darling?"

Alan could hear the impatience in his sister-in-law's voice as she complied. He joined with the others in response.

"So, Alan, you have a favorite question you want to ask?" asked Libby.

This was a loaded question. He wanted to ask each person at the table why they'd abandoned Deb and him for a whole year following their babies' deaths. He wanted to ask how they could have been so heartless and still say they believe in God.

Instead, he said. "I've always preferred the *wicked child*."

Leah rolled her eyes. "We already read that one."

"Let him read, dammit!" said Deb. Then she flushed and covered her mouth.

"It's all right. Go ahead and read, Alan."

Alan cleared his throat. "'The wicked child asks: What does this service mean to you?'"

Before the rest of the participants could give the answer, Jacob raised his hand. "Grandma, I want to read!"

Libby gave him a beatific smile. "Go ahead, sweetheart."

"'Since this child does not want to be included in the celebration, we must answer harshly: 'We celebrate Passover because of what God did for us. If you had been in Egypt, you would not have been included when Adonai freed us from slavery.'"

"Good job, Jacob," said his mom.

"How come you like the wicked child best, Uncle Alan?" asked the boy.

Alan looked at Deb and said, "Nobody should be punished for asking a question."

Amy, Alan's niece, spoke up. "But the wicked child acts like he doesn't care about the answer. He separates himself from his parents."

Deb spoke up. "Great point! When a child acts out, it's a teaching moment, not a moment to be harsh. Underneath his tough exterior, this child does seek an answer. He yearns to be accepted for who he is, not treated like the black sheep of his family."

Leah glanced at her watch. "We've already wasted fifteen minutes and we haven't even gotten to the plagues yet."

"Sometimes, plagues can wait," Deb shot back.

"Parents need to *hear* their children, no matter how young or old they are; to look for the underlying meaning in their opinions and decisions," said their mother.

Deb gave her a warm smile.

"That reading passage said nothing about opinions and decisions," complained Leah.

"I did, so there!" said Libby.

Maybe his mother-in-law had changed, after all, thought Alan.

Alan's wife grinned at him from across the table.

He lived for those smiles. The irony was, he had the key to unlock those walloping smiles but guilt over removing Justin's breathing tube continued to plague him. Unfortunately, Judaism didn't allow him to blame his sins on the devil, nor rely on another to wash away his sins. He had to take responsibility for his actions, pray for God's forgiveness, and make peace with those he wronged.

Alan smiled back at his wife. If his mother-in-law could admit her mistakes, he could certainly try to unlock the door to Deb's happiness.

CHAPTER 42

SHANA

Shana blinked drops of sweat that hung from her eyelashes like *Lite Brite* bulbs.

Wrists and ankles roped and tied, she'd been helpless to do anything but bake beneath the sun's increased intensity; a preferable fate to poison ivy.

Judging by the position of the sun, it had to be at least four hours since Daniel had dropped her body at the edge of the woods. All that time, she'd lain there, screaming *help, help*; hoping an early morning jogger or walker would come upon her. Or perhaps a bird watcher who took delight in listening to the woods awaken from its slumber. Evidently, early morning joggers and bird watchers traverse safer wooded sites than those adjacent to a highway.

The sound of police sirens and fire trucks exploded in the distance. No doubt a vehicular accident involving a shitload of cars. When Shana had first started at the newspaper, she'd covered similar accidents. She'd been pregnant with Daniel at that time. All that exposure to chaos made him emotionally disturbed. No one to blame but herself.

Shana's voice had gone hoarse. Her throat felt like sandpaper. No food or drink since yesterday. She used her roped hands to massage her cramping stomach. How could she have been so arrogant to assume Daniel would accept her belligerent attitude? He'd warned her to stop asking asinine questions, but she'd kept egging him on. Did she have a death wish? If so, it was Rachel, Becca, David, and her future grandchild who would suffer the consequences.

Then again, perhaps her disappearance from their lives would be no big deal. The girls had their own lives; they no longer needed her telling them what to do. Her husband had his photography; he didn't need her to oversee him develop pictures in his dark room for eight hours at a time.

David's words floated through her brain: *Stop feeling sorry for yourself!*

He'd voiced those sentiments more than once since her retirement. This time he'd been right. Shana had been aching for an adventure, something to give her life new meaning—at least until her first grandchild's birth. However, getting kidnapped by her son had not been on her bucket list.

Shana twisted her head back and forth, attempting to slam the mosquitoes that were dancing across her sweat soaked face. She wondered if she'd still be alive when Daniel returned—unless he had no intention of gathering her up. She didn't know what to make of him. He'd forced her to confess she was his birth mother; he'd tortured her, both physically and mentally. He'd also saved her life when she suffered a full-blown panic attack—it definitely had *felt* life-threatening at the time.

Just when Shana was beginning to think her son did care, he dumped her here in the woods to die under the scorching sun, with only a sliver of shade the trees provided.

He'd positioned her body where she'd be easily found, dead from heatstroke.

Truth whispered in Shana's ear: she was disposable. Her son didn't need her to ID her rapist; he'd researched his birth father's identity before even kidnapping her. Her heart quickened. What if he'd already murdered him? Surely, he'd want to boast of the news.

Shana began to fantasize: What if her son did come back for her, and she was alive to see him again? She'd hold him close, tell him she loved him unconditionally. He'd promise to never again commit a violent act. She'd promise to not report him to the police. She'd bring him home to meet the family. They'd accept his redemption.

Reveling in these fuzzy thoughts, Shana noticed a little girl clutching a red parasol skip past her. *Wait!* She called out, her voice grating like a cheese slicer.

The little girl in the red coat stopped to gaze at her.

Shana held up her roped arms. *Untie me, please!*

The little girl in the red hat looked at her sadly.

Go get your mommy or daddy to come help me!

The little girl in the red dress shoes unclenched her fist.

The red parasol disappeared into the cloudless sky.

The little girl skipped away.

"No!" Shana cried into the void.

Chapter 43

DEBORAH
DECEMBER 1984

Deborah's family would be ringing the bell anytime now. What a relief that Chanukah and Christmas Eve both fell on the same night this year! Her niece and nephew wouldn't be sulking about how unfair it was that they couldn't have a tree.

She worked alongside Alan, placing the potato latkes he'd fried onto a festive serving platter. "This second batch is too oily. We need another paper towel to pat them down."

Her husband thrust the roll of paper towels into her arms. "There you go!"

"Very funny." She pulled a single towel off the roll to absorb the excess olive oil.

Alan wiped his sweaty forehead with his apron. "You think I should put more grated onions in the next batch?"

"It's cool the way you did it." Unlike her, he couldn't savor the smell of sautéed potato and onion pancakes.

Deborah opened the oven to check on the chicken. Um. The smell of paprika was tantalizing. She turned the temperature to simmer.

This year, Leah was bringing the matzo ball soup, and her mother, a homemade honey cake. Deborah was filled with gratitude. With her new position as director of the synagogue's preschool program, Deborah would never have had the time or energy to put it all together. But this year, everybody was helping. Even Alan's brother Jerry, who believed Chanukah was just for kids, had deemed tonight's dinner worthy of attending.

Alan turned off the stove. "All done." Deborah followed him in the utility room and watched as he rolled his dirty apron into a ball and tossed it into the hamper. "Hole in one!"

She grabbed him around the waist. "My hero."

Alan moved her hands away. "Now you got my shirt oily!"

"No big deal," she said, reaching for a spray bottle on the shelf. Normally, she was the one who demanded cleanliness, but tonight she was too revved to care.

They dressed for dinner. "You've been more affectionate lately. What's up?"

"I've been feeling happier since I went back to work."

"So that's it?"

"You've been a lot more helpful with cooking and cleaning, too."

He looked up from the mirror after straightening his tie. "If I was a less discerning man, I'd accept your words, end of story. But something tells me my Deb isn't telling me everything. Come on, what gives?"

She gave him a little smile as she curled her hair. "Now's not the time. They're going to be here any minute."

He placed his hands on her shoulders and looked her in the eyes. "They can wait. Really, what's going on with you?"

"Our name finally came up on the adoption list!" she blurted.

Alan sank to the bed mattress. "What?"

"A five year old boy, born right here in Chicago!"

She pulled a Kodak picture from beneath their bed. "Check it out! Brown hair, brown eyes, just like you!"

"He's a handsome kid. Why would somebody give him up?"

"Evidently, he was adopted at birth by an interfaith couple, but four years in, the wife died of cancer and the dad couldn't cope. The boy's been in a foster home for the last year. He was brought back to DCFS."

"Temper tantrums are par for the course for that age," said Alan. "Jerry and I acted out a lot when we were young. There's more to this story, trust me."

Deborah fidgeted with the pillow sham. "There was evidence of physical abuse. Burns that went unexplained. Neglect. Food anxiety."

"I don't know, Deb. Sounds like this kid has hard core behavior problems."

She put her arms around his neck. "I deal with behavioral issues of our preschoolers; some issues are more serious than others. I'm fully equipped to handle his challenges and get him the help he needs."

Bing, bing.

Alan stood. "They're here."

Together, they headed toward the front door. "Can we at least meet him?"

"I guess," he said.

Deborah did a happy dance.

"What's that all about?"

"We've got an appointment with the boy and his social worker tomorrow."

Chapter 44

SHANA

Shana awoke to something bumping against her. "What the fuck!" she croaked, straining to come to a sitting position.

"Are you a frog?" asked the straggly haired women in the garbage bag cape.

"Why did you kick me?"

"I'm a frog, too." The woman pointed deeper into the forest. "Me and my little ones live down there, next to the pond. Thought you were dead, lying on your back like that. Looks like you've been out of the water too long. Lucky for you, your body's still moist! Didn't want you to get run over by a bike, so I bumped you. Once I got my neck stuck in a plastic circular thing people throw away. Thought I was a goner. But all the frogs came to help me, even some tadpoles, and you know that never happens. A couple of them died because they got tangled up, too, but they were very brave."

First the little girl with the red parasol, then a talking frog. Heat stroke will soon have all of her mind. In desperation, Shana reached for frog woman's arm.

The woman hopped backward. "Nobody touches my legs!"

"Sorry," Shana said. "Thanks for bumping me away from danger."

"Toads can endure brief touch," frog woman continued, her eyes bulging, "You crave touch, so you must be a toad."

Shana felt herself drifting in and out of consciousness. She struggled to get her words out. "Cell phone? Call kids, tell where am."

Ribbit, ribbit. "Only humans have cell phones, silly."

"Find phone human throw away?" Shana asked desperately.

"Where's the pond you and your polliwogs are staying at?"

Was she really conversing with a frog, wondered Shana. Had she turned into a frog, too? Shana attempted to verbalize these questions, but her words refused to leave the womb.

"Didn't mean to get into your business by asking a personal question," said frog woman.

Shana grimaced as she recalled the personal questions she'd asked in the two-and-a-half decades she'd been a reporter.

"Okay, then. Let you get back to your polliwogs. Good hopping!"

"No go!" Only the woods heard Shana's hoarse screech.

Alone again.

Skin hot.

Raw.

She closed her eyes

and

waited

for

death.

Chapter 45

DETECTIVE HERNANDEZ

"This is me," the suspect responded pleasantly.

Detective Hernandez placed the first of three camera surveillance pictures on the table before him. "And this?"

Aamer leaned forward in the conference room chair and glanced at the three pictures, one by one. "All me."

"Did Shana know you were following her?" the detective asked.

Aamer straightened his red tie. "I do not believe."

"Your wife told Becca you left the restaurant early to make a flower delivery."

"True."

"So you delivered flowers to a customer. What is this customer's name?"

"I not remember. You talk to boss. She will tell you."

"What time did you deliver the flowers?"

Aamer checked his cell phone calendar. "I arrive Sunday, twelve-forty."

"And what time did you leave the restaurant brunch?"

He leaned back in his chair and looked at the ceiling. "Twelve-ten p.m. I pick flowers up from store, then bring flowers to people's houses."

"Where did you go after you delivered the flowers?" asked the detective.

"No more deliveries, so I return to restaurant. Shana ran outside. She look very unhappy. I worry for her, so I follow."

"Did you catch up with Shana?"

He looked perplexed. "She didn't need ketchup."

Smiling in spite of herself, she rephrased her question. "Did you speak to Shana?"

He shook his head. "She far ahead."

"Did she see you?"

"I not want to embarrass her."

"What was your plan?"

He looked at her quizzically.

"You say you were following her, correct?"

"I stay far behind for long time."

"So you didn't want to talk to her, and you didn't stand near her."

Aamer nodded.

"Then what was your purpose? Why did you follow her?"

"She not have purse or phone. I not want her to get lost, and nobody there to help. So I try to help."

"You were being a good Samaritan."

Aamer shrugged. "I not know this word."

The detective tapped her shoes impatiently. "You were being a good guy."

He smiled widely. "Yes, a good guy."

"When did you first meet Shana?"

"Sunday a.m. This was first time I see Zander, my step-son, in many years. He invite me to be with family at restaurant. While we wait, Shana, daughter Becca, and I talk."

"How did Shana act toward you?"

"Sorry?"

"Was she friendly? Mean?"

"She hug me, very happy to meet me."

"Then what happened?"

He opened his arms wide. "She ask me many questions."

"What did she ask you?"

"Where I grow up? How life was when I was little boy? When I come to United States?"

"How did you like those questions?"

"It make me happy to talk about long ago. Many good memories."

"Did Shana ask you any questions you didn't like?"

Aamer nodded, his smile slightly dimmed. "She ask why ISIS fight and Koran love. I smile at her, but this question make me cry inside. Becca sad, too. She fall, but I pick her up."

"Then what happened?"

"Red light buzz. We all go in restaurant." Aamer stood. "I very tired, need to go home now."

The detective stood, wide stance. "I will tell you when and if you're going home tonight."

Aamer gave her a puzzled look.

"Just a few more questions."

Aamer smiled. "I answer good, then I go home."

"When it began to rain and thunder at the Park, did you help Shana?"

Aamer shook his head. "I have no umbrella. But tall young man have umbrella. His shoes look like alligator. Shana step under umbrella. I leave."

"Did she seem happy to go with the young man?"

"She quick go under umbrella, no problem."

"Last question."

Aamer put his hands in prayer position.

"You have a cell phone. Why didn't you contact your step-son when you saw Shana was in distress?"

Aamer looked down at the table. "Zander not give me his phone number."

"Did you phone your wife?"

Aamer brought his palms to his eyes. "I not want worry my wife, so I follow Shana. Now she is dead."

"We don't know that yet. The police artist will sketch your description of the young man with the umbrella. Then I will release you."

"Thank Allah!" Aamer reached across the desk to hug her, but the detective pulled her gun on him.

Aamer eyed the gun and raised his hands, terror in his eyes. "You not kill me, please!"

She returned the gun to its holster. Then she moved toward him slowly, handcuffs in hand. "No one's going to hurt you, Sir. Clasp your hands behind your back."

"What mean…?"

"Do it!" she shouted.

Aamer froze. "I am U.S. citizen. Wallet in pants pocket. You see!"

"Hands behind you, Sir!"

Aamer moved his hands behind his back. As she cuffed him, sweat poured from his forehead.

The detective used her phone to photograph the suspect; then she punched in the number to the global security database. Stepping away from Aamer, she turned and spoke into the phone. After a few minutes, she returned her phone to her pocket. "You might want to call your wife. Looks like you'll be spending the night here, after all."

Chapter 46

SHANA

Shana's eyes opened woozily as she felt herself being lifted, then flung over someone's shoulder. Her unroped legs bopped in the humid breeze, and her chin banged against a scratchy chest, as he hauled her down through the gravel road.

"Son?" she mumbled through parched lips. Faint with hunger, thirst, and sun stroke, she wondered if he was rescuing her or taking her deeper into the forest.

He grunted with her weight. "Evidently, no one figured you were worth rescuing."

Rescue. He was going to rescue her, she dizzily rejoiced.

He looked both ways, then roughly unloaded her body onto a park bench. He pulled a water bottle from his backpack, squeezed open her lips, and poured the liquid down her throat. Not slow, not fast, but in a steady stream.

Still, she choked as she guzzled the water. "F-food?"

He broke off chunks of a trail mix bar and fed them to her slowly.

A guttural sound escaped her lips, asking him to untie the wrists.

"After the day I've had, you really don't want to piss me off." His gaze fell to the sunburn molts covering her body. "You need medical attention."

He was taking her to the hospital! "I no tell," she attempted to eke out.

He sat back on his haunches. "There is no one to tell!"

Her eyes widened.

"You thought I was taking you to the hospital? That's not going to happen. See, I'm still trying to decide if I should let you live or die. Playing God, if you will. Actually, it's kind of an exhilarating experience. That said, I'm no monster. I'll do what I can to relieve your discomfort." He dug in his bag for a cold pack, then crushed it to activate. "Here you go," he said, placing the cold pack on her forehead.

Shana's eyes shone with gratitude.

"Bet you're wondering whether I visited Daddy Dearest without you."

She blinked once.

He placed two pills on her tongue and gave her a sip of water.

She looked at him warily. "Wha…?"

"Antihistamines to reduce itching and swelling. I staked out his house, just like they do in the movies. He pulled into the driveway at 3:15 p.m. He lifted a set of golf clubs from his car trunk—he drives a Mercedes—and started into his garage.

"It was then I confronted him. He asked my name and purpose. I came right out and told him I was his son. He dismissed my claim. 'I've been a bachelor my whole life. Never fathered a kid. Family slows a man down. My job kept me traveling all over the world. More than enough excitement for me.' He gave me his best wishes and turned to go into the house.

"I said 'wait,' fished out my cellphone, and showed him your yearbook picture. 'Am I supposed to know this person?' he asked.

"This is a picture of the woman you raped in college. I am your son from that union.

"Despite my reminding him of the frat party he attended at the end of senior year, the booze, the dancing, the barbiturates he put in your drink, Daddy continued to deny responsibility. You know how strongly I feel about accepting responsibility for one's actions, don't you?"

Shana felt herself fading off again.

He opened a popsicle box and stuck a lime pop between her lips. Then he placed her roped hands on the popsicle stick. "There you go. In case you're wondering, these ice pops are organic. No sugar added. Shall I go on with my story?"

Her throat threatened to shut down at the propelled object, but the lime taste began to massage her taste buds.

She blinked once.

"Daddy told me how sorry he was, but that I had the wrong man. He shook my hand and turned back to the door. I reached over his shoulder and stuck him in the heart with a knife. You remember the pocketknife I slashed across your cheek when you first came to visit?"

Shana moaned.

"Yep, it was one and the same. Did you know a pocketknife can inflict an immense amount of damage if you use it effectively?"

Shana spit out the popsicle. It fell to the gravel below.

Daniel's eyes blazed. "I give you water and food. I nurse you back to health, and you have the audacity to fling it back in my face?"

Just then, a bicyclist stopped abruptly. "Heard screaming. Are you guys all right?"

Before they could answer, the cyclist's eyes fell to Shana's roped wrists. He jumped off his bike. "Holy shit. What happened?"

"I was jogging by when I came upon this woman. Her wrists were roped, her whole body sunburned. Thought she had sunstroke. I'm a medic so I've been administering first aid and giving her food and drink."

"Did you call an ambulance?"

"I called about thirty minutes ago, but there's been a ton of car accidents today, so the ambulances are all in service."

"Got your car here?"

"I live a little over a mile away, so I usually jog over. Couldn't move her, anyway. Not in her condition."

The cyclist laid his bike against a tree and knelt by Shana's head. "You okay, ma'am?"

Here was her chance to be rescued. Shana willed herself to respond. "Ugh."

The cyclist stood. "Let me give 911 another go." He punched the numbers into his cell and spoke into the phone. "Okay. They'll be here in ten minutes."

"Listen, dude, I'm late for work. Could you possibly chill with her until they arrive?"

"No problem," said the cyclist.

They shook hands.

The cyclist's fingers paused over his cellphone keyboard. "Just need your contact information for when they ask me what happened."

"Yep, my name is Rod Stewart, 1355 5th Avenue, 312-666-2101."

Shana moaned.

The cyclist glanced at her. "Hang tight, ma'am. The paramedics are on their way." Then he turned back to Daniel. "It must be tough being named after a singing legend."

Daniel laughed. "My dad really enjoyed his music. Unfortunately, I can't hold a tune."

"So this phone number. Not a New York area code, huh?"

"I moved here from Chicago couple of weeks ago."

"Killer place to live!" said the cyclist.

Hearing his words, Shana forced a louder moan from her lips.

"I look forward to checking it out."

"By the way, my name's Gabe Rider."

"At least *your* name makes sense! Listen, thanks again. Tell the fire department she's had food, drink, and 50 milligrams of antihistamines within the last thirty minutes."

Gabe glanced at his cellphone watch. "It's six-thirty now. Okay, got it. Hey, don't work too hard tonight."

Without a backward glance, Daniel waved goodbye and jogged off into the distance.

DAY 3

CHAPTER 47

RACHEL

Hey, Becca. Zander's mom just posted bail for Aamer. She said he was bawling all the way back to their apartment.

OMG Rach! Why did they even keep him overnight?

Detective Hernandez was all set to release him, when he tried to give her a bear hug. She put him in cuffs.

No way!

Aamer got agitated, so the detective checked the global security database. His name appeared on a No Fly List.

He's a terrorist??

Aamer's last name is Abdelrahman, but the name in the database is Abdelraman, like the noodles.

BTW, Ramen is spelled with an e, not an a.

Thanks teacher.

Thanks sculptor.

Turned out to be one big miscommunication.

No more bear hugs to police from Aamer.

Mom gives bear hugs!

Mom won't be on a terrorist list anytime soon.

You sure about that?

Aamer should file a complaint against Detective Hernandez.

She's just doing her job, Bec.

Did U know seventy-three percent of U.S. terrorist attacks have been carried out by white nationalists living in this country?

No politics, please.

White supremacists!

Stop, Becca! Right now we need to focus on getting Mom back, safe and sound. Gotta go. Nurse is here to take my blood.

Sorry for upsetting you earlier.

No worries. I'm feeling much better. Just do what you gotta do on social media to bring Mom home.

Chapter 48

ALAN
JANUARY 1985

Today marked two years since the babies died. Alan tried to delete that day from his mind as he watched the five-year-old year chase the cascade of soap bubbles Deb was blowing through her wand. The adoption counselor sat beside Alan on the park bench, clapping appreciatively. This was the third time he and Deb had met with the home study counselor over the last few months, and it looked like today would be their lucky day.

"Come play, Alan!" Deb had started a new game; she zigzagged across the field, clutching a big rubber ball as the preschooler chased her.

The counselor gave Alan an encouraging look, and he knew it would look good on today's observational notes, so he did what came unnaturally and ran toward them. As a child, Alan couldn't recall ever playing ball with his dad, who was always working, reading, or napping.

Of course, he'd played Tag with his niece and nephew; on rare occasions he'd even pushed them on the swings at the playground. But the truth was, he'd never learned how to *play*. How could you be a good dad if you didn't know how to play?

The ball smacked him in the chest. "Pay attention, big guy!" Deb called.

Alan prepared to throw the ball back to her. "Me! Me!" yelled the child.

Alan twirled the rubber ball on his finger—wow, he didn't even know he could do that—then tossed it to the kid.

"More! More!" cried the boy.

Alan gazed into the boy's laughing eyes. Then he tossed him the red ball.

Deb ran up to him. "He likes you! You're going to be a great dad!" She grabbed the ball from the child and tossed it across the field.

Together, they watched him run to retrieve it.

"How can you be so sure? All I've done with him so far is read, color, light Chanukah candles, watch Mr. Rogers, share Crunchy Crunch cereal, and play a little ball. Doesn't seem like we know each other yet. I'm not sure he even likes me."

Deb brought her forehead to his. "Honey, you've got doubts. I do, too! But even Rabbi Shapiro says it's time for us to move on with our lives. Start a new family. Wouldn't it be a beautiful testament to our babies if we adopt this little guy on the anniversary of their death?"

"Don't we have more paperwork we need to fill out?"

Deb placed her hands on her hips. "Alan Stewart, are you going to cop out on me?"

"Can't a guy ask a simple question without getting bludgeoned to death?"

She planted a big smooch on his lips. "It's just last-minute jitters, like you got before we walked down the aisle."

"I should have taken those jitters to heart," he said wryly.

A streak of pain crossed her eyes.

"Kidding! I'm blessed to have you in my life. Who else would nag me all the time?"

"Maybe it really is too soon," his wife said hesitantly.

Alan dabbed her tears away with his fingers. "Today we start a new family!"

Deb looked up at him. "Are you sure? It's not going to be easy raising a kid with abuse and abandonment issues. Research shows fifty percent of marriages end in divorce; adoption is one of the causes."

The boy ran up to Alan and handed him the ball. "Throw, Daddy, throw!"

The ball fell from Alan's hands. His face felt hot. Tears traveled down his cheeks. He picked up the child and held him close to his chest.

Deb threw her arms around both of them. "Is that a 'yes,'?"

"Yes!" said Alan.

"Yes!" said the child.

Their child.

Their son.

Chapter 49

SHANA

"Mom?"

Shana squinted into the brightly lit room. "Where am I?"

"You're in the hospital," said her younger daughter. "A bicyclist found you in the woods. Thank God you're all right!"

She glanced at the transparent tape covering the needle in her hand, then the tube running up an IV pole. Her heart began to pound. "Why am I here?"

"You were totally dehydrated and suffering from heatstroke. The doctor said it's a miracle you survived."

Shana looked at the bandages covering her wrists. "Did I attempt to kill myself?" she asked incredulously.

"We thought you could tell us that," said a voice she didn't recognize.

She looked towards the voice. "Who are you?"

"I'm Detective Hernandez and I've been handling your case."

Shana's eyes glistened with fear. "What case?"

David's face came into view. "You disappeared three-and-a-half days ago, hon."

"Where did I go?"

"That's what we want to know," said the detective.

It was then she noticed her older daughter Rachel in a wheelchair. "Oh my God. What happened?"

She saw a look pass between her husband and daughter. "The doctor put me on bedrest."

Shana's arms tingled. "Why?"

Bzz, bzz.

A nurse hurried into the hospital room to check Shana's heart monitor. Frowning, she tightened a blood pressure cuff around Shana's arm.

Shana cringed, then glanced at the nurse's name tag. "Katrina, can you please loosen this thing?"

Becca's eyes twinkled. "I see you're definitely back in action!" Shana tried to match her daughter's expression, but a fleeting memory of another cuff sped through her brain.

The nurse peeled the blood pressure cuff from Shana's arm. "Your mom needs to be stress-free so she can fully recuperate."

"I'll be stress-free once you tell me what's going on here."

The nurse gave her a perfunctory nod and exited the room.

"What is the last thing you remember before being rescued?" asked Detective Hernandez.

Shana closed her eyes to visualize. "Our family was eating brunch at a restaurant in Central Park. The girls and I got into an argument and I dashed out of the restaurant."

"Do you and your daughters argue often?"

"Every now and then. But nothing like this."

"With mom, it's always something," said Rachel. "She routinely asks waiters to turn down the air, or if she can have a grapefruit slice in her ice water. This time, I had to loan her my cardigan sweater because she forgot to bring her own. She knows restaurants are going to be cold when it's 90 degrees outside."

Detective Hernandez turned toward Shana. "That the straw that broke the camel's back?"

The nurse came back in to recheck Shana's blood pressure. This time her nod was authentic as she left the room.

When Shana didn't respond, Becca burst in. "Mom was upset because I got on her case about asking Aamer personal questions about his political and religious beliefs. That was before we even set foot in the restaurant."

"I don't deserve to be humiliated in public by my own children..."

"... but being humiliated in private is okay?" teased Becca.

"After you left the restaurant, where did you go?" asked the detective.

"Why all these questions? Speaking of questions, is the baby okay, Rachel? Is that why you're here?"

Her older daughter glared at her. "Now you care about how we're doing. Sure didn't show it when you took off on your own in a city you've never been to before."

Shana felt weary with disappointment. "Rachel, do you trust me that little? I'd never do something like that, especially with you being pregnant!"

"I told the girls there was no way," said her husband.

"So where *did* you go?" asked Becca.

Shana signaled David for a glass of water. She took a sip. "I was furious. I planned to catch an Uber back to the hotel, then book a flight home to Goldsboro. But then I remembered my phone was dead and my purse was back at the hotel. A horse & carriage driver offered to drive me to the Park exit for free, but I couldn't recall which of the four entrances we came in. I couldn't even remember the name of our hotel!"

"What do I always say?" asked David.

"Photoshoot street crossings and monuments in case you get lost and don't have your GPS handy," said Shana. "Kind of tricky to take pics when your cell phone's dead, though."

"You've always got an excuse," said Rachel.

"Stop arguing, guys," said Becca.

"What happened next?" asked the detective.

"A young mom let me call Rachel on her cell phone, but when she answered, I hung up."

"Why?" asked Rachel.

"Because I knew you and Becca would never let me live it down."

"No lie," Becca said wryly.

Shana grimaced. "I'm exhausted. I need to rest."

"Just a couple more questions," said the detective.

"If you're too tired, the detective's questions can wait," David said firmly.

A wave of love for her husband washed over her. It had taken years, but he was finally standing up for her. Still, she waved off his concern. "I'm okay."

"After you hung up, what did you do?" asked the detective.

"I was dripping with sweat. It began to storm. All the visitors hurried from the park, but I reveled in the twenty-degree temperature drop, and the refreshing rain pounding my body."

"Were you carrying an umbrella?" asked the detective.

Shana shook her head. "Fortunately, a tall young man offered his oversized black umbrella. I remember telling him I raised you girls to view strangers as friends you've not yet met. I stepped underneath the umbrella. Then everything went blank."

"Did you catch a glimpse of his face?" asked the detective.

"Thin. Tall. White. Dressed nice. Twinkle in his eye."

The detective placed the Park photos before her. "Does this man look familiar?"

As Shana gazed at the photos, her gut instinct urged her to lie. But this would be way more than a little white lie.

"I need an answer."

David arose from his chair, cane in hand. "My wife needs a nap. Perhaps we can resume this conversation later."

The detective headed for the door. "Count on it."

Chapter 50

DEBORAH
FEBRUARY 1985

That first night Deborah held Daniel in her arms, she sensed something amiss. His fuzzy words—the words he'd captivated them with that afternoon in the park—had made them a family. The child's unbridled joy in running, playing, and laughing; these emotions were real. But that first night, and those that followed, he'd wake up shrieking like a burn victim; inconsolable for hours.

Deborah had plugged a moon-faced night light in his room. When Daniel began pinching his arms. Deborah held him close to her heart. "You're okay, you're okay," she murmured.

When cuddling failed to calm the boy, Alan insisted they bring him to the pediatrician. But at the last minute, Deborah cancelled their appointment. "It's only been two weeks, Alan," she pleaded. "Daniel is just settling in. He needs to know we're here for him, that we're not going to abandon him."

They agreed to postpone the doctor's appointment until further notice. *Further notice* crept into their son's bed at

3:14 a.m. The night before, her husband had stuck neon stars on the ceiling above Daniel's bed.

Deborah was dozing in the rocking chair, as she'd been doing since the night they'd brought Daniel home, when a piercing shriek clawed the silence. She jumped from her chair and rushed to her son's bed. It was then that she saw the long red streaked wounds. The blood under his nails. Steeling herself against the sight of her little boy's self-inflicted horror, Deborah lifted him from his bed and carried him down the hall into the master bedroom. "Alan! Wake up!"

Her husband shot up in bed. "What happened?"

Their son began to shriek.

"Daniel's hurt himself. We need to get him to Emergency!"

◇◇◇◇◇◇◇◇◇

The doctor finished bandaging their son's arms. "These wounds look mighty deep for a five-year-old to inflict upon himself."

"He's really strong for a little kid!" Alan agreed.

Deborah's radar kicked in. "What are you trying to say, doctor?"

Alan had tried to reassure her. "He's just commenting on Daniel's strength."

"Doctor?" she repeated.

The doctor perused their file. "It says here you and your husband adopted Daniel earlier this month. That you lost three babies two years ago."

"It's not like we misplaced them," said Alan, his expression dour.

Her husband was clueless. Deborah knew what the doctor was insinuating. She waited for him to spell it out.

"Losing one baby, let alone three, can be very traumatic, resulting in PTSD. The parent replays the scenario over and over again. Sometimes unintentional actions can result."

"What kind of unintentional reactions?" asked Alan.

"The kind where you carve up your child's arms," Deborah said brusquely.

"Calm down, Mrs. Stewart, I'm not inferring you harmed your Daniel."

"If I used a kitchen knife, I could have done a more efficient job of it."

"Deb!"

"I work in the childcare field. You're a mandatory reporter, just like me. You must report suspected child abuse."

"That's crazy, Deb. The doctor isn't going to report us."

The doctor cleared his throat. "Actually, I must."

Alan looked incredulous. "But we've done nothing wrong! We knew when we brought Daniel home from DCFS that he'd experienced abuse and neglect while in foster care."

Deborah's heart filled with pride as she listened to her husband stand up for them. "We tried for three years to get pregnant with no success," Alan continued. "Do you know what that does to a young couple? Do you know what that does to their faith in God?

"Then I found out my sperm was for shit; my wife required a donor to impregnate her. Do you know how worthless that makes a man feel? The jocks used to tease me in high school because I was six-feet, two- inches and couldn't make a basket! My mother wouldn't let me play football because she was scared I'd get brain damage. Brain damage would have been better than going through four years of hell."

Deborah laid her hand on his shoulder. "Honey, it's okay."

Alan thrust her hand away. "It's not okay, 'cause God wasn't finished with us yet. He had to send us three babies, two dead in utero but delivered, and a third, Justin was his name. He lived one week before I pulled the plug. Yep, doc, I pulled the plug on my own baby because his organs were irreversibly damaged. He couldn't breathe on his own. What kind of life is that for a child? For the siblings yet to be born?"

The words tumbled out as if a dam had broken inside him. As if he couldn't stop even if he wanted to. "It was actually a relief, yes, a relief, to unhook Justin's breathing tube. After what my wife and I have gone through, I knew with all certainty that should he have miraculously live, Deborah and I could never have endured raising a severely disabled child."

The doctor's shocked expression matched Deborah's own. She thought she and Alan had been on the same page, releasing Justin from needless suffering before his certain death. Alan had never mentioned a secondary motive for unhooking Justin from life support. It cast their baby's death in a different light. Could Justin have been saved? Did she really know this man at all? She swallowed the lump in her throat and steeled her resolve.

Although she was devastated at this new development, Deborah knew the next few minutes would determine their future as parents. She wasn't going to let anyone stand in the way of keeping this child.

She looked over at her husband. At 6 ft. 4 inches, Alan was at least five inches taller than the doctor. She wondered if Alan was manic enough to kill him. "Come on, Alan," she said, her voice soothing. "Let's take Daniel and get out of here."

"About that...," said the doctor.

"You think we physically injured our son?" Alan asked incredulously. "This child, who, even with his fucked up behavioral issues, is our hope? Our redemption? All we want to do is love him. Heal him."

The doctor's eyes grew hard. "Heal him?"

"We're not talking cults, here," Deborah snapped. "With God's help, we will heal Daniel by caring for his emotional and physical needs, setting limits, and rewarding positive behavior. Unconditional love, that's what a child needs to feel *whole*."

"But you admitted to killing your other baby," said the doctor.

"Doctor," Deborah said carefully, praying that her words were true, "my husband expressed his guilt over a selfish thought he experienced at the time of our baby's death, but this was secondary to the compassion he showed toward the baby while he still lived. Our doctor and rabbi can vouch for this. Is it really so unusual for a parent to feel relieved when such a severe obstacle has been removed? We are, in fact, only human."

The doctor pondered her comments, then offered them a sad smile. "Daniel's emotional and physical well-being is all that concerns me. If, in fact, it is Daniel who inflicted these wounds upon himself, it's going to take a lifetime to heal this child."

"There's an old African proverb, doctor," said Deborah. "'It takes a village to raise a child.'"

The doctor put his hands on theirs. "I am risking my license by not reporting the two of you and giving you a second chance. Don't make me regret it."

Chapter 51

SHANA

The lead smell of blood assaulted her nostrils. Her eyes widened in fear.

She attempted to scream, but her vocal chords had been severed. As flames engulfed her, the words shot through the top of her head. My Child!

Ahh! Shana awoke, her body trembling.

David put his book down and enfolded her in his arms. "You're okay, you're okay."

Shana looked wildly around her. "Where am I?"

Detective Hernandez strolled into the room. She stared at Shana's face. "Looks like your nap didn't go so well."

"She had a bad dream," said David, smoothing the hair from her face.

"It wasn't a dream!"

The nurse rushed in to once-again check Shana's heart monitor and blood pressure. "I'll be right back with something to calm you down," she told her.

"Maybe you'd like to share it, this dream of yours," said the detective.

"No stress," David reminded the detective.

"A monster was slashing me over and over again. I froze. Couldn't move. Flames all around. I burned to death."

David rocked her in his arms. "Poor Darling."

"Your left cheek does have a slash mark scar."

Shana raised her hand to her cheek in surprise.

"Detective, if you're going to upset my wife, you'll need to leave."

Detective Hernandez raised her hands in resignation. "Gotcha. Where's your kids?"

"We didn't know how long Shana would nap, so we had Rachel wheeled back to her hospital room. Becca went back to the hotel."

"Must be costing you a mint to be staying at the Roosevelt all this time," the detective observed.

Shana's face brightened. "So that's the name of our hotel!"

Her husband looked at her quizzically.

"I wanted to go back to the hotel but couldn't recall which U.S. president it was named after! My cell phone died, so I couldn't Google it."

"So you said," remarked the detective.

"I was furious with myself for forgetting to bring the phone charger along with me to brunch."

"Did you notice anybody following you at the park?"

She shook her head. "I was focused on finding an exit."

"There's map boards all over Central Park."

The nurse came back into the room and tinkered with Shana's IV bag. "There you go. Have a nice visit." Then she left the room.

"We need to get her a nice gift for being so kind," mused Shana.

"Map boards, Mrs. Kahn," said the detective, a slight edge to her voice.

"I'm not good at reading maps."

The detective flipped through her notes. "You were a reporter, right?"

"I grew up in Chicago, so I didn't need maps to get around."

Detective Hernandez once again produced her photos. "Do you recognize the person holding the umbrella?"

Shana glanced at the pictures. She gulped air. "My monster."

"Detective, I warned you."

"Is this the monster who gave you those rope burns on your wrists and ankles?"

Shana nodded.

"Detective, I demand that you…." interrupted David.

"The same monster who slashed your cheek?"

"Yes!" Her scream felt refreshing, emboldened.

David shook his cane at the detective.

Shana placed her hand on his. "I have to help the detective kill the monster!"

"Nobody's going to kill anybody," said the detective.

"But you must. He already killed my rapist."

David sank into his chair. "Rapist?"

Shana remembered once reading a Gloria Steinem quote: *The truth will set you free, but first it will piss you off.* So what if she was doing it in reverse order. "It was a week before college graduation. I'd just gotten hired as a reporter for the *Chicago Sun-Times*."

She noted the stony expression on David's face. "You weren't even onboard at the Newspaper yet!"

"Whatever."

"I celebrated by going to a frat party. Danced all night. Disco. Strobe lights. D.J. Got drunk. Went to the bathroom. Came out. He put a roofie in my drink. Next morning, I woke up in a strange bed, naked. Wet. Smelling of semen."

"Did you report the rape?" asked the detective.

Shana squeezed her eyes. "It was the '80s. Female victims were blamed 99 percent of the time. My reputation would be in the toilet. This was my first real job."

"So your answer would be 'no'?"

Shana glanced at David. "I was so drunk, I didn't even know my rapist's name, let alone the name of his fraternity."

"Why did your 'monster' want him dead?"

A spark of memory flew through her brain, but her mental tweezers were unable to grasp it. "Maybe he saw himself as an avenging angel."

"What was the connection between you, your monster, and your rapist?"

Another spark, this second one almost invisible. "No clue."

Shana glanced at David. He was biting his lower lip, a familiar facial expression that signaled his disgust to her *little white lies*. He'd never understood that a reporter had to do what she had to do to get results. This time, though, Shana had no clue what that truth was.

"Do you know the identity of your 'monster'?"

A butterfly of a name hovered just above Shana's head, but when she attempted to catch it, the butterfly fluttered past. Shana's thoughts drifted back to the woods, her captor looming over her, a bicyclist stopping to offer help to them both. Another name came to her. Although it felt off somehow, she knew both the detective and her husband needed an answer. She took a deep breath, then exhaled. "Rod Stewart," she said forcefully. "My monster's name is Rod Stewart!"

CHAPTER 52

ALAN
SEPTEMBER 1990

"Today you start fifth grade. How do you feel about that?" Alan was videotaping his son, just as he'd done in years past on this day of celebration.

Daniel tossed his cereal spoon into the air. "Excited! I'm a big kid now."

Last night, Deborah had worried about him over that very fact. "Daniel's tall for his age, but his maturity level isn't that of a normal ten-year-old. Boys with winter birthdays play catch up throughout their school years. They're always the youngest in the class. Their eye-hand coordination, gross-motor skills, social skills, spelling skills, reading skills often lag behind the other kids."

Alan had been on the same page as his wife, regarding kindergarten. They planned to do Montessori—a multisensory program that enables a child to explore learning at his or her own pace—for the one year between pre-school and kindergarten. But in the end, they had acceded to the school counselor's assurance that holding such a bright boy as Daniel back a year would be detrimental to his self-esteem. They'd learned the hard way to follow their gut instinct.

Alan continued filming rather than stopping to clean the milk and Cheerios mess on the wall. "What do you hope to learn this year, Daniel?"

His son gulped his remaining drops of orange juice. "I want to learn how to read good, write good, and play kickball! I want to make friends, too!"

The blinking red light signaled the video camera battery was about to die. "Last question. How do you plan to accomplish all these great things, Daniel?"

His son jumped up from the table and grabbed his new backpack. "Listen to my teacher. Use my library voice in class. Talk, don't hit. Let's go, Dad!"

Alan zipped the mini-video recorder back in its pouch. "Got your lunch bag?"

"Got it, Dad. Come on!"

"All right. Let's do this!"

By the time Alan reached the front door, his son was already half-way down the street. "Wait up!" he yelled into the falling autumn leaves.

The crossing guard was holding out her arm for his son to wait while cars passed.

Seconds later, Alan caught up to them. "Hey, bud. We talked about this. You can't just run out of the house like an airplane on fire!"

Daniel began to guffaw. "Airplane on fire. That's funny, Dad."

As they crossed the street together, Alan prayed this school year would go better than last year. Wishful thinking.

Chapter 53

DETECTIVE HERNANDEZ

Detective Hernandez chuckled at Shana Kahn's lame attempt to insert humor into her investigation. "Rod Stewart, huh?"

Shana shook her head impatiently. "My kidnapper was way taller and younger than the classic rock singer."

Thanks to the bicyclist who'd found Shana, Hernandez already was privy to the kidnapper's description, including the alligator-patterned high tops, but she wanted to confirm whether or not their stories meshed. "What kind of shoes was he wearing?"

Shana burst out laughing. "He didn't wear shoes during my bondage, detective."

"Did he reveal any other personal information about himself?"

Kahn seemed to consider her question. "I heard him tell the bicyclist who discovered us in the woods that he'd been jogging when he found me lying there. He also said he was a medic and had to get to work."

"What time of day did this occur?"

Shana appeared to be fishing for a memory. "The sun was going down. I must have laid there for several hours because my skin felt raw, and my mouth tasted like stale French bread."

"How did you get to the woods?"

She stared up at the ceiling over her hospital bed. "I remember my wrists and ankles being bound."

"Was Stewart the person who bound you?" continued the detective.

Shana gave a quick nod. "He threw me in the back seat of a fancy black car. Said we were going on a field trip."

"Where to?"

"I don't know!"

"Take it slow, detective."

The detective observed Shana flutter her eyes at her husband. Looks like she appreciated this new and improved model.

"No problem," said the detective. "What do you remember about the car ride?"

"We drove for a long time."

"Freeway? Gravel road?"

"Smooth road. Driving fast. It was freezing inside the car. I asked him to turn off the air conditioner. That's when he pulled to the side of the road and hauled me into the woods. He dropped me on the blacktop trail. Said he'd be back for me that evening if the wild animals didn't get me first. Then he left."

Shana began to sob. The detective handed her a tissue.

David Kahn frowned. "You seriously need to stop!"

"Shut up!" said his wife. "I'm doing this!"

Her husband heavily came to his feet, grabbed his cane, and stalked out of the room.

"I'm such a bitch."

"You're upset. Your husband will understand."

"Poor guy's taken forty years of my shit."

"It takes two to tango, they say," said Hernandez.

"True that!"

The detective poured her a glass of cool water. "Did anybody come upon you while you were lying in the woods?"

Kahn stared up at the ceiling again. Then she said, "A little girl dressed in a red coat, red hat, red shoes. She was skipping down the path, carrying a red parasol."

The detective's eyes narrowed. No parent would dress their kid that way with the temperature clocking in at ninety degrees. "Was the little girl with somebody?"

"She was all alone. Weird, don't you think?"

The whole story was weird, thought Hernandez. "What time of day did you see her?"

This time, the woman answered without hesitation. "The sun was straight overhead, so it had to be around noon."

"Did she talk to you, or you to her?"

"I pleaded with her to help me, but she just let go of her red parasol and skipped away."

Hernandez noticed the victim's faraway gaze. If she had been left in the sun all morning, dehydrated, she could be hallucinating. "Anybody else stop to help you?"

"It must have been a workday, because nobody passed me for hours. I thought I was dying. Then a homeless frog woman stopped to chat. She was dressed in a big plastic cape."

The detective glanced up from her notes to see if she was joking, but the woman's facial expression was solemn. "Her polliwogs were waiting for her at a nearby pond. She asked me which pond my polliwogs and I were staying.

"I said I didn't know. Then I asked her to untie my ropes. The frog woman laughed. 'Frogs don't use scissors!' Then she left."

That Shana took seriously her encounter with the frog lady was a bad sign. Hernandez stood and placed her notebook in her pocket. She felt the need to somehow comfort this woman. "It's not unusual to hallucinate following trauma and dehydration."

"I am not hallucinating," Kahn said harshly, "but I am done answering your questions. Please tell my husband to come back in now."

Hernandez shook her head in frustration as she exited the room.

Chapter 54

DAVID

David remained on the hospital bench, uninclined to rejoin his wife in her room. On one hand, Shana's bitchy words signaled she was back in good form. On the other hand, the few days he'd spent apart from his volatile woman—the few nights he'd spent away from her since she'd retired—had been a blessing. The horror of not knowing if she was dead or alive? He wouldn't wish those feelings on Jack the Ripper himself.

Still, it had been a huge relief to not have to account for every decision he made, no matter how minute. He'd deepened the bond with his daughters through collaborating on finding their mother. The abject loneliness he'd experienced sleeping without his soulmate, not knowing whether his would be a temporary or permanent occurrence. All these experiences had taught him that no matter what transpired, he could make it on his own.

Which was why he didn't hobble right back into his wife's clutches. Especially after she'd humiliated him in front of the detective. Now that Shana had returned to him, safe and sound, disconcerting thoughts flooded his brain: Stay married to the woman he'd loved for a lifetime or cut painful ties instead. Become a hermit far away from her and their daughters or be present for the birth of his first grandchild. Could he really sever ties with his family at such a life-changing moment as this?

Perhaps these crazy thoughts sprang from enduring the shock of his wife's disappearance, coupled with the ongoing health of his daughter and grandbaby. Then there was the rape, itself. The rape Shana had unilaterally chosen to keep hidden from him for forty-two years! He'd discovered his treasure chest filled with worms rather than gold coins. Good enough reason to call it quits.

"Sir, your wife is asking for you," said a bookmobile volunteer.

"Thank you." First the detective, now the volunteer. With a deep sigh, David slowly came to his feet, grabbed his cane, and headed down the long hall toward his wife's room.

◈◈◈◈◈◈◈◈◈

As soon as David entered her room, Shana began to apologize. "Honey, I'm sorry about overreacting. I know you were trying to protect me, but I'm capable of handling things myself."

"Fine."

"What's wrong?"

David abhorred conflict. He changed the subject. "How did the Detective's interrogation go after I left?"

"Detective Hernandez wasn't interrogating me; she needs to get all the facts so she can find my kidnapper. It's funny. You think a bad guy's going to be dressed like criminals on

T.V., but Rod was dressed in a lovely summer suit. That's why I felt confident enough to share his umbrella."

"Did the detective mention a police artist coming to take your description of this guy?"

"Maybe I could give you the description instead," she said, pursing her lips.

David was not in the mood. "I'm a photographer, not an artist."

"But you minored in art when you were in school."

"Have you ever seen me pick up a sketching pad or easel?"

Shana placed her palms over her eyes. "I can't think straight anymore."

"It's going to take a minute for you to recuperate from this trauma."

She peeked at him through her fingers. "'Take a minute!' You sound like a homegrown North Carolinian!"

David rolled his eyes.

Shana turned serious. "It's strange. Detective Hernandez doesn't believe what I tell her."

"Like what?"

She dropped her hands back in her lap. "Like when I mentioned chatting with a homeless frog woman about her polliwogs."

Chapter 55

DEBORAH
MARCH 1994

"You certainly weren't perfect when you were Daniel's age!"

Deborah wiped her hands on a kitchen towel. "Sometimes I wish we didn't make up."

Libby huffed. "Well, that's a nice way to talk to your mother!"

Deborah immediately went into guilt mode. But this was one time she wasn't caving. "Daniel is 14 years old. He's not a little kid anymore! He knows right from wrong. But you continue to explain away his mistakes."

Pound. Pound, Pulsating.

"Turn that X-Box down, Daniel!"

The pulsating ceased.

"How many times did God excuse our mistakes?" her mother persisted.

"For sure, but we're talking Daniel, here, not Moses!"

"You're forgetting *Daniel and the Lion's Den*."

"Very funny."

"I thought so!"

"Every time I confide in you about Daniel's destructive behavior, you blame it on his foster care experience. Especially the skin graft after being burned."

"Unbelievable an adult would do that to a child."

"Of course it is, but we can't attribute everything to his past. We've raised him since he was five years old. We've given him play therapy, set up behavior mod charts to reward positive behavior, placed him in support groups for abused children. He sees a language arts tutor, plays sports, and goes to Hebrew school."

"Darling, you and Alan have done a beautiful job raising your young man."

"We've done such a beautiful job that our son set fire to another kid's gym shoes because the kid was bullying him."

"What goes around comes around."

"He's been suspended from school three times since fourth grade!"

"I certainly don't have all the answers, sweetheart. Otherwise, I'd have figured out how to hold on to your father."

Deborah grunted her assent.

"What I do know is that making Daniel think he's *broken*, frantically trying to *cure* him, hasn't worked."

"How arrogant I was to believe that just because I'm a preschool teacher, I'd know how to raise a troubled little boy."

"He needs unconditional love. Hold him. Praise him for deeds well done, no matter how minute."

Deborah began to weep. "We've done that since the day we brought him home from DCFS. You know we did!"

Her mother held her close. "God only gives us what we can handle."

She broke from her mother's arms. "We paid off any debts we owed God when He took our three babies. He's not getting our fourth one, too!"

"You're feeling overwhelmed. Let me make you a nice hot cup of herbal tea."

Deborah hugged her chest. "This summer, we're sending Daniel to Camp Ramah in the Rockies. They have an outward-bound wilderness camp where they do rafting, backpacking, and camping. Daniel will learn to be independent, to work as a team player, and to actualize his Jewish identity."

The annoying pounding and pulsating resumed. "Turn it down!"

Daniel swung open his bedroom door and ran toward her. He thrust his headset in her hands. "Put this on. You won't hear a thing."

Deborah thrust the headset back at him. "You're the one who should be wearing this."

He threw the headset to the floor. "Leave me alone!" Then he raced back to his room.

"I made some homemade cookies for you, darling," Libby called after him.

S-L-A-M!

Deborah stalked down the hall and pounded on her son's door. "Bubbe doesn't deserve that rude behavior. No dessert tonight."

"I don't care!" he yelled through the door.

Castigating herself for getting into a shouting match, she headed back to the kitchen.

"Don't be so hard on yourself and Daniel," said her mother. "He's almost a pre-teen. That's how they act. This overnight camp sounds interesting, but he's had problems adjusting to day camp. Won't he feel that you're abandoning him?"

"That's what Alan says," Deborah admitted.

Libby raised her eyebrows.

"He wants to take Daniel on a fishing trip this summer, instead."

Her mother looked at her quizzically. "I didn't know Alan was into that sort of thing."

"He's not. His father never did any cool things with him when he was growing up. Just work, work, work all the time. His mother took him to boy scouts, but that only lasted one year. Alan's just not an outdoorsy kind of guy."

Libby set the herbal tea bags on the kitchen table. "Sounds like Alan's bonding plan is a fantasy."

She gave her mother a sharp look. "He and Daniel are closer than Daniel and me."

"Leah was always daddy's little girl and you were always mine."

Deborah dangled a bag of raspberry tea in her cup of boiling water. "Maybe if we'd adopted a brother or sister for Daniel, things would have worked out better."

Libby poured herself a cup of tea. "That's unlikely," she said gently.

Deborah put her cup down a bit too harshly. Red stains covered her place mat. "What are you saying?"

"I'd tell you, but I'm afraid you'll banish me from your life again."

"Wait a minute! Who banished whom? And at a time when I desperately needed you?"

"Daniel's violent tendencies might have had serious consequences."

"I can't believe you're talking this way about your own grandson!"

"That's the reason Leah doesn't allow Amy and Jacob to come over."

Deborah frowned. "Leah never mentioned a problem."

"Don't pretend you didn't know."

She shrugged. "What Leah decides to do or not do with her children is not my business!"

Daniel sheepishly took a seat at the kitchen table. "Sorry I acted like a jerk."

"Language!" said Deborah.

"Okay, okay. Sorry. Can I have some cookies now?"

"Say 'please,'" said Deborah.

Daniel grinned at his mother and grandmother. "Please!"

"Anything for you, dear," said his grandmother.

Kids these days! Deborah rolled her eyes, but her lips were smiling.

Chapter 56

BECCA

Becca was in bed watching T.V. when she heard her dad swipe the hotel room card and walk into her room. His face looked *morose*. She'd need to remember to incorporate that word into a drama class lesson when school resumed in the fall.

"Sorry to leave you alone in the room all this time."

"No problem. I've been watching a show about NYC. Not that we'll be doing the tourist thing anytime soon."

Her dad took a diet pop from the minifridge. "Want anything to drink?" he asked.

Becca pointed to her bottled water. "How did it go with Detective Hernandez and Mom?"

Her dad took a seat on the double bed across from hers. "It was rough going. Mom got emotional. The nurse gave her something to calm her down. Medication made her sleepy, so the Detective had to hang out in the waiting room while Mom napped."

"So what *did* Mom tell the detective?"

"She talked about what happened just prior to the kidnapping and after she was released. Detective Hernandez will question her again tomorrow."

"Was Mom able to give the detective any personal information on her captor?"

Dad massaged the bald spot on his head. "His name is Rod Stewart."

"OMG. Like the classic rock star?"

He gave a small smile. "It turns out the guy is a medic who lives within jogging distance of the woods where he dumped Mom. He moved here a couple of weeks ago from Chicago."

"Whoa! Did Mom know him?"

"Not sure."

"What's the next step?"

"A police artist will sketch mom's description of this Rod fellow. They'll put that sketch on TV and Facebook. See if they get a hit."

Becca let out a relieved sigh. "At least they've got a plan."

Her dad still seemed unsettled. "Is there something else?" she asked.

"I'm not sure we can trust mom's account of what happened to her."

Becca raised her eyebrows. "Why?"

"She mentioned talking to a frog woman about her polliwogs," he blurted.

She giggled. "You know mom's a jokester."

"She was dead serious."

"She's got a dry sense of humor, Daddy. Remember the time she tried to convince me and Rachel you were the Wizard of Oz?"

He grinned. "Go to sleep, I'll read in the other room."

"Night! Love you!" They'd used that same bedtime phrase since she could remember.

"Love you, too," he said. Then he shut the door between them.

◇◇◇◇◇◇◇◇◇

As soon as her dad left the room, Becca texted her sister. *What's going on?*

Zan just went back to Oma's apartment. How's Mom?

First, how are you feeling?

Better. Guess I really did need to slow down.

Becca recounted the conversation she'd had with Dad.

Mom might have PTSD.

That's for soldiers and abused kids.

Maybe she was tortured after she was kidnapped. She could be blocking horrific memories. A trigger could set her off.

Rach!!

"You okay, Bec?" Dad called from the living room.

Shit. Gotta go.

Becca clicked off the phone.

Chapter 57

DANIEL
APRIL 1997

Who could have guessed it? His face on the cover of the *Lerner News*. Being recognized as a hero couldn't have come too soon, considering the trouble Daniel had been having since starting high school last fall.

For the last three summers, his parents had sent him off to wilderness camp in the Rockies. At first, he thought they were just trying to get rid of him. Daniel had acted out that first summer of overnight camp, hoping to get himself sent home, but the counselors had been cool about it. They told him all the conflicting emotions he was feeling were normal, which came as a big surprise. He thought he was the only person in the world to feel sad, angry, or lonely.

At camp, Daniel learned how to be friends with other kids his age instead of bullying or being bullied by them. From mountain climbing and zip lining, he learned to trust his fellow campers and camp counselors. Most of all, he learned there were good people whom he could depend on, who had his back.

Daniel felt better about himself; he even began to clean up his act at home, doing the chores his parents requested of him. Being polite at the dinner table. Teaching his dad how to shoot baskets with him on the weekends.

Even his teachers had shown Daniel a new respect. When he made insightful comments on *The Chronicles of Narnia* or wrote a persuasive essay on why the New York Yankees finally won the World Series after an eighteen-year dry spell, his teachers' eyes would shine with pride. In eighth grade, Daniel had hit it out of the park on the University of Chicago School Mathematics Project, with high schools vying for his registration two years in advance.

Just as Daniel was beginning to accept happiness and calm as his due, his camp counselor phoned to let him know that Lucia, the girlfriend he'd hung around with freshman year that summer, had fallen off a mountain. She'd survived, but her body was in full cast and she was in a coma.

Although his mom and dad offered to cover his flight, Daniel refused to travel to Montana to see her. Once again, his thoughts grew dark and cold. He stayed holed up in his bedroom, the shades drawn. Sophmore year had been a bust; he missed 54 days in a row. Thanks to home tutoring provided by the school district, plus the fact that he was a good test taker, Daniel had passed. Last fall, thinking their son could use a change of scene, his parents enrolled him in the Chicago Math & Science Academy, a high ranked charter school and one of the schools vying for him.

But CMSA turned out to have a lot more Brainiac students in its junior class than Daniel had anticipated. Once again, negative thoughts burrowed in his brain; he was worthless, stupid, friendless. Concerned about his downward spiral, his parents picked open his bedroom door lock and read his most recent poems which talked about suicide. They dragged him to a private shrink, the one he'd seen years ago to get him on medication. But this time, nothing worked. He was sinking into the pit of hell, and his parents were on the same elevator.

Daniel asked Rabbi Shapiro to convince his parents not to admit him to Rush Behavioral for a six-week in-patient program, but the Rabbi agreed with his parents that hospitalization would be beneficial.

The day before he was scheduled to be admitted, Daniel prayed to God nonstop. "Help me find another way," he begged, "and I'll devote my life to you."

Later that afternoon, he'd been hiking through the frozen ice framed by Lake Shore Drive when he heard a scream. "Help!"

He looked in the direction the sound came from. A wide black hole sat amidst the frozen lake. Someone was bopping up and down through the hole. "Can't swim!"

Daniel didn't think twice. He shrugged off his coat and boots on the icy sand and swam into the frigid Lake.

"My body's getting numb! Help!"

Using the competitive breast stroke he'd learned at camp, Daniel drew nearer to the person who so desperately required his help. He grabbed a wool hat with a white pom-pom floating on the lake's surface and held it up for the girl to see—no doubt it was hers. Then he placed one arm around the teen's waist and paddled them back to shore using the side stroke.

Although Daniel tried his hardest to keep the girl's head above water, she slipped a few times. Her face had a blue tinge as he laid her body on the frozen ice. Pinching her nostrils, he attempted CPR. Two breaths, compress, two breaths, compress. Finally, her eyes flew open. Her arms had wrapped around him. "My hero." Then she'd drifted back into unconsciousness.

Thank God cell phones had come on the market earlier this year. Daniel retrieved his phone from his coat and punched in 911.

After the newspaper article came out with his picture and the girl's story on the front page, there was no more talk of hospitals and rehab centers. God had granted him his wish. Now it was Daniel's turn to uphold his part of the bargain and rescue those who needed rescuing.

DAY 4

Chapter 58

DETECTIVE HERNANDEZ

"You were a bit hazy last night. I need you to give me more specific details about your time in the woods."

Shana Kahn sat propped up in her hospital bed, munching scrambled eggs and a toast with grape jelly. "My captor fed me this menu!"

"Mrs. Kahn, you need to focus so we can find your kidnapper," the Detective said impatiently.

A memory dot came to mind, causing Shana to swing the food table arm away from her bed. "Rod threw a plate of eggs in my face. The eggs fell to the floor and got mixed with my poo."

Was this an encore of last night's hallucinations, or new evidence, Hernandez wondered. Better to treat it as valid than have her superiors kick her in the butt for not doing a thorough investigation. "Where were you at the time of these meals?"

"Rod's grandmother's house. She was dead, though. He said he didn't kill her, but I'm pretty sure he was lying."

Hernandez had put the police artist sketch on hold, requesting a shrink come interview Kahn first, but Dr. Poinsetta couldn't make it until noon. Kahn's husband and kids hadn't come to visit yet, so she had the woman all to herself. "What makes you think he's not telling the truth about his grandmother's death?"

"I don't even know if she *was* his grandmother. The house was vacant, and Rod said it was up for sale. He could have broken into the house and taken it hostage, too."

Hernandez had to concede she had a good point. "Any broken windows or doors?"

"No, but he could have come down the chimney, like Santa Claus!"

So much for valid points, thought the detective. "Do you remember driving far from Central Park when he first kidnapped you?"

Kahn groaned. "Rod thinks I have Alzheimer's, but your memory's a lot worse than mine, Detective. I already told you I remember nothing between feeling a bee sting on my thigh and freaking out when I found myself chained to a radiator pipe."

"More likely a Diazepam injection than a bee sting."

"You and Rod can enjoy a good chat about drugs. He's a medic, you know."

The detective noticed Kahn seemed not to realize she'd shared that information the night before. "Did he say where he works?"

"He told the bicyclist about a multi-vehicle collision on the expressway—I know you people call it *freeway*—and how he had to get to work, second shift. So maybe the local fire department?"

Hernandez had already checked it out. No one by the name of Rodney Stewart, Rodem Stewart, Romey Stewart, or any Stewart worked there. Also, no listing for any Stewart living within jogging distance of the wooded area where Shana Kahn was found. Nor were there any nearby homes within ten miles of the crime scene sporting a *For Sale* sign. Suddenly, the detective experienced an *ah ha* moment. "You said your captor told the bicyclist that he'd jogged to the woods."

Kahn nodded as she spread jelly on a second slice of toast.

"You also mentioned that he hauled you over his shoulder to bring you back to his car."

Kahn looked confused.

"Roped and tied you in the back seat of a black car. Drove for a long time."

Kahn nodded.

"Which means your captor wasn't holding you hostage at a site within jogging distance."

Kahn raised a juice glass to her lips. "I never said the house was near the woods."

Hernandez was exasperated. "There's only apartments, condos, and hotels in close proximity to Central Park, unless this *house* was actually an apartment or condo!"

Kahn glared at her. "My thoughts might be hazy, but I'm pretty sure I can tell the difference between a condo and a single-family dwelling."

"Mrs. Kahn, we're going around in circles, here."

"That's because you're making me crazy with all your questions!"

"Probably how people felt when you interviewed them for your newspaper articles," the detective observed wryly.

"What are you talking about?"

"You were a reporter, right?"

"Now you *have* gone bonkers. I worked as a flight attendant for American Airlines."

The detective put her head in her arms.

Kahn's eyes widened. "Did I make you sad?"

Hernandez stood and started for the door. "I'll be back at noon with another visitor."

Shana Kahn excitedly slammed her juice glass down. "Frog-woman and her polliwogs?"

Hernandez raised her head skyward, then left the room.

Chapter 59

ALAN
MAY 2001

Alan retreated to the backyard, slamming the door on his wife's ranting and raving. He paced the weed-strewn lawn, his thoughts incongruous with the joyous bird tweets echoing from the fern tree branches. Never in his wildest nightmares would he have imagined his loving wife, the mother of his son, being diagnosed with early Alzheimer's. The symptoms were as nasty as those experienced by eighty-year-old nursing home patients.

It had been nine months since Deborah had begun confusing time and place. She repeatedly asked the whereabouts of her *blankie*. She'd been fired from her teaching job for allowing a preschooler to consume a bite of watermelon, even though his file specifically listed the fruit under *allergic*.

Even more stressful was her difficulty in performing routine tasks. She'd spread margarine across her forehead instead of on toast. Pull her socks up her arms and run outside naked; the latter being the straw that broke Daniel's back. Their son spent marginal time at home, which was a shame, since high school graduation was in twelve days.

Alan and Deborah had planned for their son to graduate from Princeton University, majoring in engineering. He'd been fortunate to have received a full-boat scholarship for all four years, which had really eased their pocketbook.

But life hadn't turned out as they'd planned. Deborah's two-year life expectancy, coupled with his own precarious hold on his engineering job, necessitated Daniel stepping in to help care for his mom.

With a heavy heart, Alan had broached the subject to his son at breakfast that morning. The resultant blow-up was not unexpected.

"Are you really asking me to take a hiatus from college—again?" screamed Daniel.

Alan had successfully managed to conceal information about their babies. Neither he nor Deb had wanted Daniel to view himself as a consolation prize. As he listened to his son carry on like an idiot, he seriously regretted their decision.

"We're talking about your mother, for God's sake! The woman who's been there for you, through all your mishegoss! Six months of your life. That's all I'm asking. Then I can retire early, receive my pension and not have to pawn your mother off on hourly workers."

"I repeat, Dad. I am not living in this house, and watching Mom deteriorate!"

"You know this isn't your fault, right? Mom has a disease."

"You're right. It's not my fault. That's why I'm getting the hell out of here."

"Language, Daniel! She needs you!"

Duffel bag in hand, Daniel held the screen door ajar. "Don't you get it, dad?" he lamented. "I love her too much to watch her disappear. She doesn't recognize me most of the time, as it is."

"I know it's difficult for you, just as it is for me."

Daniel swiped at his wet cheeks. "I'm going to be late for my flight. Take care. The vroom of the gas pedal from the Camaro, followed by silence.

Watching his son's car pull away from the house, Alan felt empty, like a gas pump that had exhaled its last drop of gas.

With a deep sigh, Alan viewed their house with tired eyes. The place was in total disarray since Alan had to watch his wife as soon as he came in the door after work. Dirty clothes overflowed the hamper. Cracker crumbs dotted the living room carpet like stars in the galaxy. The pantry was bare for lack of time to shop for foods that would keep his wife's bowels working without causing triggering her Crohn's Disease; a condition she'd recently developed. To make matters worse, Alan was up half the night making sure Deborah didn't turn on the kitchen stove or jump out the window.

"You need to buy child safety locks, like you did when Daniel was small," his mother-in-law urged, as she did every day he came home to relieve her of her post.

But Alan had hesitated to act; he was in a state of denial, just as he'd been twenty years before when his three infants had chosen immortality with God over mortal life with him and Deborah. Her disease was just a bad dream, he tried to convince himself. Soon he'd have the love of his life back the way she'd been: Warm, vibrant, in charge.

The truth was, he'd become accustomed to Deborah scheduling his life, just as his mother had done for him and his father until her death. He cringed to think he would fade into a shadow of a man, as had his father.

The screen door swung open. Alan looked up in surprise to see his son burst into the kitchen. "What are you doing back?"

"I have a question."

Chapter 60

BECCA

Becca laid the black and white striped journal on the hospital bed. "For you, Mommy."

Mom picked up the journal. "Really?"

"Unless you'd prefer I give it to Rach."

Mom clutched the journal to her chest. "This means so much, Bec. I've missed being able to confide my thoughts and feelings on paper, especially about my kidnapping."

Becca felt a twinge of jealousy. "I'm always here for you."

"I appreciate that, Darling, but my memories are too muddled to share out loud."

"Dad says you gave Detective Hernandez a lot of information about your captor."

Mom flipped through the empty pages. "I feel like there's a lot more I've suppressed. That's pretty common among trauma victims."

That she acknowledged her trauma was a positive. "Some things are too painful to revisit. That's why I let my students choose whether or not to re-enact traumatic events in their lives."

"I hope you have a therapist waiting in the wings!"

"Knew I forgot something!"

"Do you realize the liability you face if one of your students has a panic attack or later commits suicide?"

"The college has liability insurance."

"You obviously don't remember the college professor I interviewed who was sued because he gave an 'A' student an 'F' on her final exam. The girl had a nervous breakdown."

"Spoiler alert. My students use body language to portray positive emotions, too."

"That's a relief!"

"Your memory seems to be right on point, though."

"It's my short-term memory that's dangling in la-la land."

"There's trauma you're unwilling to dredge up, Mommy. Trauma that can enable Detective Hernandez to bring your captor to justice."

"You've been watching too much *Law & Order SUV*."

Becca laughed at her mother's comic substitution for SVU. But she refused to be distracted. "Were you sexually abused by Rod?"

"Hello! He cleaned my nude body when I was sitting in shit, then covered me with a kitchen towel. He was definitely gay."

Becca looked down at her hands. "Or you were too old to turn him on."

"Thanks for sharing!"

"You were held hostage for two days. What did you guys talk about?"

"Food, water, power, control. Unshackling me from the kitchen radiator. Cleaning up my poo and pee."

Definitely TMI, thought Becca. "We also talked about Facebook. He spied on your posts, as well as Rachel's."

Becca's face felt hot. "Rach and I never friended a guy with that name."

"But people can lurk on Facebook, right? Read your posts without you even knowing?"

It looked like she'd underestimated her Mom's social media prowess. "We changed our settings to 'private.'"

"Not soon enough!"

"He had to have a motive."

Becca noted her mom had that *staring through you* expression going on; the expression she got when she was trying to summon up a memory. This time, she wondered if it was an authentic memory she was summoning.

"Rod thought I was friends with a college guy who raped his girlfriend. He wanted revenge."

Becca heaved a sigh of relief. "Sounds like a definite connection."

Mom glanced at the ceiling. "Another name has been pricking my brain, but it flits away before I can catch it. I feel like this is the real name of the person who kidnapped me."

Becca's heart began to pound. "Are you saying Rod Stewart is not your kidnapper?"

Mom shook her head. "It's Rod's body, but *Rod* is not his name."

As Becca tried to process this latest development, her mom continued. "What if Rod didn't really move to New York? What if he still lives in Chicago and flew here to kidnap me?"

"Why wouldn't he just kidnap you in Chicago?"

"Maybe he knew from social media that I'd moved to North Carolina."

"How are we going to find this guy? There's gotta be hundreds of Chicago residents with the last name of 'Stewart,' unless Stewart is his *first* name."

Her mom turned her head away. "Stop! These 'what ifs' are giving me a headache."

"You started it. If he's lying about that, maybe he's lying about being a medic."

"Then he is a really good actor because he knew the correct medical procedures to follow for someone with sunstroke. He also knew the ER doctor needed to be told when I'd last consumed food and water, as well as what medication I'd recently taken."

"You can find all that information on You Tube."

"Let's assume Stewart is Rod's actual last name. Criminals prefer to change their first name; their surname keeps them connected to their personal universe."

"Okay."

"What career could he have if he's adept at Facebook and You Tube?"

"That's hard to say. Everybody and his mother knows how to use computers today."

"Not me! I just watched a *Sixty Minutes* segment about Facebook privacy."

"Yeah, well that's you. People in their 80s and 90s are all over social media."

"I'm not old enough to know that, yet."

"What does that even mean?"

Mom waved her hand dismissively. "Don't go off on a tangent."

"Aye, aye, Captain!"

"If he is working with computers, what facet would he be in?"

"The way he planned everything out so carefully, I'd guess something high level, like surveillance."

"Maybe he's one of those brains behind home security cameras that allow you to see who's at your front door, even though you're at work."

"Well aren't you becoming tech savvy," Becca teased.

"Thanks to all the TV commercials I've been forced to watch on hospital TV," Mom says wryly.

Then it hit her. "Maybe Stewart does computer surveillance."

Her mom stared at her. This time her expression is clear and bright. "I remember him telling me that!"

Becca rejoiced at this driblet of memory. "Let's call Detective Hernandez."

Mom scowled. "She doesn't believe a word I say."

"Maybe she can take our information over the phone."

"And maybe unicorns don't fly."

"They don't. They're not real."

"Ha, like frog women can't talk!"

Becca glanced up to see if she was pranking her.

Her mother's solemn expression convinced her otherwise.

CHAPTER 61

DANIEL
MAY 2002

Daniel made himself a peanut butter and banana sandwich and went to his room to sulk. Today he should have graduated Princeton University with his class. Soon after, he would have begun a fantastic career in computer engineering making six figures to start.

And it was all because of HER.

He'd succeeded in convincing his dad to let him return to Princeton for fall semester, promising that if his mom's health worsened, he would come back home the following semester.

Daniel had been hedging his bets. He knew that, when push came to shove, his father would never allow him to miss the last few months of his senior year, especially when he learned that his son had already been approached by two prospective employers. A fact he'd elected to keep to himself. A reminder that his future was way more than his mother's hallucinations.

Yet, despite his protests, there was no way he would turn his back on his mother, the woman who had been there for him every step of his life. He owed her big time. He would be there for her after he got his degree.

That had been his plan.

Doomed from the start.

As Daniel bit into the gooey sandwich, his mind filled with memories of going off to college for the first time. Although his dad, in his quiet, measured way, did his best to make Daniel's college transition a positive one, it had been bittersweet without his mom there to cheer him on. But her medical condition prohibited her from flying, let alone enduring the 12-hour drive from Chicago to New Jersey.

It took a while for Daniel to acclimate to living away from home. Before she'd developed Alzheimer's, his mom had cooked for him, picked out his clothes, and most important, believed in him. When he repeatedly fucked up in high school, his mom had advocated for the school to put him on a 504 plan to resolve his behavior problems.

Intellectually, Daniel knew he was not to blame for his mother's medical condition, nor the Crohn's Disease that followed—his dad had repeatedly drummed that into his head. But deep down, he couldn't help wondering if the stress he'd caused her had precipitated her plunge into a living hell.

Halfway through first semester, Allie had walked into his life and assuaged his fears. One of only ten female students in his graduating class, Allie was brilliant, nerdy, and gorgeous. Best of all she loved him, which she consistently demonstrated through the next two years of college.

Despite his dad's protests, Daniel had stopped going home for holidays and vacations, choosing instead to hang with Allie and her family at their summer home or winter cabin. He'd just about convinced himself that life was moving on a upward trajectory when, in June before his senior year, he received the phone call he'd dreaded.

"Daniel," his father had said, "I'm sorry to do this to you, but you've got to come home. Mom's gotten a lot worse, and I can't work and take care of her with only Bubbe to help."

"Why can't Aunt Leah and her kids help?"

"It's not their job, son."

"Put her in a nursing home," he pleaded.

"Would you want us to give up on you if, God forbid, you had a terminal illness?"

"But I'm doing great at school. I'm dating a nice Jewish girl. That's what you guys always wanted, right?"

"You can always go back to school, son, but your mother is not always going to be here."

Daniel knew he was being a jerk, but some evil spirit was urging him on. "I have a right to live my own life. I've got a scholarship for my whole college career. I'm not leaving."

His father sighed on the other end of the line.

Prickles of guilt edged through Daniel's resolve, but he held firm. "Mom won't even recognize me if I come home."

"She doesn't recognize me anymore, either."

The sound of his dad's sorrow was tearing him up inside. "You can get a nurse or companion to help you out."

"Your mom's too young for Medicare, where those services would be covered. I'd have to pay out of pocket."

"You always boast about how well the stock market's doing."

"The experts are predicting a recession in the next couple of years," said his dad.

Daniel warned himself to remain steadfast in his resolve. "That's then, this is now."

"Come home, son. You can finish up school at ITT."

"But dad…"

His father's voice hardened. "I'm not going to beg. You're over 18. I trust you to make the right decision."

Daniel heard the click.

⋄⋄⋄⋄⋄⋄⋄⋄⋄

On the flight home, Daniel had wept non-stop. When the stewardess asked if he needed anything, he retorted: "I need my mother to be normal again. Can you give me that?" She'd scooted away. "Didn't think so," he called after her. The passenger in the seat next to his followed the stewardess' example, the seat remaining empty for the remainder of the trip.

Allie had offered to return with him to Chicago. For the summer, but Daniel knew in his gut—though he refused to admit it aloud—that summer vacation could stretch into the fall. He loved Allie too much to allow her to risk school and career. She tried to convince him otherwise, they'd argued, and he'd left on a sour note.

⋄⋄⋄⋄⋄⋄⋄⋄⋄

Daniel had still been in a foul mood when his dad had clicked off the ignition. Silently, he'd followed his dad up the driveway and through the kitchen door.

He remembered his shock at seeing his mother for the first time in several months; her skeletal body, her expressionless face. Bits of scrambled eggs dribbled from her lips, a soiled bib catching the mess.

Dad had grabbed a baby wipe and lovingly drawn it across her lips. "Sorry you have to see your mom this way."

Daniel had dashed from the room, slamming his bedroom door behind him.

His life as he knew it was over.

Chapter 62

SHANA

Dr. Poinsetta excused herself to use the visitor bathroom down the hall. Shana glanced at the wall clock above the television. Twenty-seven minutes. That's how long she'd been talking to the shrink about what happened during her bondage. Although the police-appointed psychiatrist reacted compassionately to her story, Shana sensed the doctor, like Detective Hernandez, believed she was withholding the real name of her captor.

She certainly wasn't going to confide the conversation she'd had with her daughter, that she sensed her captor went by another name, because she could be wrong. Hell, she'd told the detective she was an airline stewardess! Her memory was *slowly* returning, but it was still too faulty to rely on.

Even if Shana's memory returned to normal, how many times in her newspaper career had she misinterpreted the body language of her interviewees, placing a negative spin on their words? Fortunately, the editors caught her innuendos before publishing her articles.

Shana was attempting to put into words the visual images that floated through her brain, but it was damn difficult to capture them all. She'd told the psychiatrist about being chained to the kitchen radiator, about the overpowering smell of ammonia her captor had used to mop away her poo. The plates of food he'd flung in her face. The ever-present hunger and thirst. Her terrifying fear he'd carve her into beef stew if she didn't do as he directed.

And still, the psychiatrist sought more from her; more than she could give.

Dr. Poinsetta resumed her seat across from Shana's bedside. "Did Rod tell you why he kidnapped you?"

The single memory was back and strong; a memory she'd not even shared with her daughter. "Rod kidnapped me to revenge my rape."

"Nineteen to twenty-seven percent of women are assaulted during their college career. Why would Rod choose to avenge your rape, specifically? And why avenge a rape that occurred almost fifty years ago?"

Shana worried she looked like an idiot in front of the shrink, but the flap covering her memory of this answer was cemented shut. "I wish I could tell you. I really don't know."

"Rod asked if you knew the name of your rapist. You told him you did not, correct?"

Shana hugged herself. "He accused me of lying. Then he hacked into the guy's telephone records."

"Rod is a medic, correct?"

Shana put her hand to her forehead. "Yes. No."

The psychiatrist looked up in askance.

Might as well tell her what she and Becca hypothesized. "My daughter and I think Rod is actually in computer surveillance."

Shana noticed Dr. Poinsetta's eyes widen. No wonder. She hadn't shared that tidbit of information with Detective Hernandez.

"What makes you think he lied about his profession?"

A flood of information flooded Shana's consciousness. "Rod said he worked for the Department of Children and Family Services in Chicago," she said, her voice bubbling over. "He tracked foster care parents to ensure children were not being abused, just like he tracked down information on my college rapist. Just like he tracked my movement upon leaving the restaurant. He saw I was without a purse or cell phone. That's how he was able to swoop in on me when the rainstorm hit. He brought an umbrella along, leaving nothing to chance."

"I feel your excitement at being able to finally put two and two together," said the psychiatrist. "However, the question remains, "Why you, Shana? Why would your captor book a flight from Chicago to New York solely to track you down, to kidnap you?"

But Shana was too psyched with sharing her newly retrieved memories to answer. "The important thing is, he did it. Rod found out where my rapist lived. Then he moved to New York City—at least that's what he told the bicyclist—and confronted the rapist."

The psychiatrist rose. "Thank you for chatting with me, Shana. I hope this time has been beneficial for you."

"Definitely! I can't wait to tell Mrs. Frog about our conversation."

At Dr. Poinsetta's tight smile, Shana giggled, another memory marble fallen into place. "Just kidding!"

"I wish you and your family the best of luck."

Shana placed her hands in prayer position and bent forward from the chest. "Nameste."

The psychiatrist pivoted. "You practice yoga?"

"I do. So does Rod."

"Really!"

Shana closed her eyes for a second. "He sat in yoga pose as he questioned me about my relationship with my daughters."

"How did he know about your daughters?" asked Dr. Poinsetta.

Shana closed her eyes again. "Facebook."

"He talked to your daughters on Facebook?"

She shook her head. "He read their Facebook posts, which is how he knew we were flying here to meet my son-in-law's family."

"Did he say how he got your daughters' names?"

"Don't know. By the way, whatever happened to the little girl with the red parasol?"

CHAPTER 63

ALAN
SEPTEMBER 2008

We've come full circle, Deb, Alan whispered to his wife as he stood over her sleeping body, preparing to remove her breathing tube. She'd been in hospice care since the beginning of the year, her death imminent. Unlike after Justin's death, Alan doubted Deborah's family would find fault with his actions. They had all paid dearly for loving this woman of his.

But Daniel had paid most dearly. Foregoing his senior year of college. His future as an engineer in limbo. Changing his mother's pull-up diapers while Alan was at work, bearing witness to his mother's retreat into infanthood, had done its damage.

Daniel had regressed into the old behaviors he'd brought with him as a young child. Distrust, acting out, self-mutilation. Older now, Daniel had hooked up with a series of prostitutes—who knew what kinds of diseases they transmitted. Nightmares were his son's constant companion. He worked out four hours per day, except on the Sabbath.

At one point, he'd introduced one prostitute as the girl he planned to rescue and marry. Fortunately, Rabbi Shapiro was able to make Daniel see the light. "Each person possesses the tools to rescue him or herself. God can help, but that person, alone, must do the work. You want to help this girl? Just be present for her."

Alan hadn't been doing so great, either. He was a wreck; his hair long and straggly, his eyes bloodshot from little sleep. Deborah had regressed into dementia; she kept him up all night with her shrieking—calling for her dead babies. Alan worked just enough hours to keep his engineering job. Lucky for him, he still had his mother-in-law to help, and his boss was very understanding. Alan knew Libby had been right all along; he should have put Deb in a nursing home. But they'd have to use up their life savings before she'd have been accepted on Medicaid. He couldn't leave his only remaining child destitute; he knew Deb would have felt the same way.

Daniel had offered to set Alan up with a Go Fund Me Facebook Account to raise money for Deborah's placement, but Alan had declined. He detested asking people for money. Even Deborah's mom and sister had been unaware of the dire straits in which they were headed.

It had taken Daniel three years to graduate ITT; two years longer than it should have. Since graduating, Daniel had once again begun to get his act together. He broke off with the ladies, cut back on extreme exercising, and was eating and sleeping better. He interned for DCFS; tracking foster care parents to make sure they were fostering for the "right" reasons had become his obsession. Not a bad obsession to have, thought Alan.

All was going in the right direction when Daniel began inquiring about his birth parents. He'd been doing so, on and off, since high school. At the time, Alan had truthfully told him he and Deborah had not been privy to that information. His son's questions had eventually tapered off—until now.

Daniel looked so despondent that Alan feared his beloved son would once again sink into a dark place. So he'd invested a few bucks in a private investigator and soon had a hit–not for Daniel's birth parents, but for his foster home mom.

"Going to meet up with her to find out why she allowed me to be abused," said Daniel.

"Slow down, dude. You need to think this through."

"I have thought it through. I need to know why my moods are so up and down."

"You're able to hold down a good job," Alan had protested.

"If it wasn't for you and mom, I'd be making $100,000 per year, instead of $9.00 per hour," Daniel grumbled.

"Yeah, whatever."

Alan winced. "Soon, DCFS will bring you on board full-time. You'll see."

"They could change their mind by then."

"What does talking to your foster care mom have to do with that?"

"Long term, Dad. I need to know where my self-loathing comes from."

Alan had been shocked. "Self-loathing?"

"Hey, it's all good. I used too strong a word. Like you say, I might be into something good at DCFS and I don't want to screw it up."

"Who are you and what have you done with my Daniel?"

"I've always been mature, Dad."

Alan kept his mouth shut. Numerous examples to the contrary.

Daniel hugged his dad. "Wish me luck."

Alan returned his hug. "Don't be surprised if this woman turns out to be a player."

"Don't be so judgmental, Dad. Maybe her husband abused her, and she was scared to stand up for me."

"Or maybe they're gold diggers who fostered you and other kids for the money."

"Relax, dad. You need to trust in the goodness of people."

Alan could not believe the words coming from Daniel's lips. His sudden change of attitude was the miracle he'd been hoping for. A new beginning.

Which was the reason Alan was delicately removing his beloved wife's breathing tube.

Chapter 64

SHANA

"Tell me the truth, David. Why is Rachel still here in the hospital?"

"Well, well," said David. "Aren't you in a feisty mood?"

Shana propped her bed straight up. "Tell me."

David lips fell into a horizontal line. "When you disappeared, the girls were beside themselves. They thought they drove you away."

"They did."

"Surely not into the hands of a kidnapper."

Shana waved her hands. "Keep talking."

"The police refused to take a report until that night, in case you'd temporarily stepped out on us."

"My bad," she said flippantly.

"You manipulated our emotions to take revenge!"

Her voice turned apologetic. "I tried calling Rachel on somebody's phone, but when she picked up, I couldn't go through with it."

"Worried your pride would take a hit?"

Shana stared into her husband's eyes. "Worried you all were so furious, you'd leave me stranded at the park."

"Sometimes it's okay to show vulnerability, you know."

Shana's eyes began to tear. "You'd all be better off without me constantly embarrassing you in public."

"So this is a pity party, hmm? 'My girls hate me. I'm so misunderstood.'"

"Save my emotional flogging for later and tell me what's going on with Rachel?"

David sighed. "While we were at the police department, her water bag broke. She was rushed to emergency."

Shana wrung her hands. "But the baby's not due for nine weeks!"

"Revenge often has unexpected consequences."

Shana felt like she'd been slapped. "You dare say that to me? How about all the times you refused to get involved, leaving me to discipline the kids, keep them on schedule, do homework with them? Passive aggressive revenge because you married a strong woman!"

David raised his hands above his head. "Don't beat me up. I'm an old man. I don't know what I'm saying."

"You know exactly what you're saying, and they're not the words I need to hear."

"It's not my fault if you can't handle the truth. It was severe stress that brought our daughter here. It's severe stress that may force her into premature labor. She's under observation for that very reason."

Shana hugged herself. "God forbid anything happens to Rachel or the baby. I've really screwed things up."

"No very much," an accented voice boomed.

She and David turned to see Aamer cross the threshold.

Shana blushed; she'd put him in the hot-seat with all her questions, and he wasn't even a criminal. At least not that she knew of. "What a nice surprise!"

"I am sorry to not come before today, but I was at police station."

Shana frowned. "Why?"

"They thought I kidnap you but find out they wrong."

"I am so sorry," said Shana.

"It is kind of you to stop by to visit my wife," said David.

"I pray hard to Allah for your safe return, and he shined his face on you."

"I appreciate that." She held out a Saltine cracker. "Sorry, this is the best snack I can offer you at the moment."

"Thank you, but I have eaten. I am more concerned with you."

"I'm great! Getting released later today if the doctor remembers to call it in."

The big, burly man looked at her uneasily. "I think that is not so great."

"Excuse me?"

"I tell police detective about tall young man with alligator shoes who take you, but he not found still, right?"

"'Yes,' I mean 'no,'" said Shana. "Rod has not been arrested yet."

Aamer removed his black hat and rubbed his bald spot. "You know this man who capture you?"

"She should, I'm her son."

The three of them looked up to find a tall young man sporting a copper-colored beard and mustache and old school wire-rimmed glasses.

Shana's jaw dropped.

David slowly rose to his feet. "My wife and I have no sons."

The young man pulled a gun on him. "I wasn't talking to you."

David put his hands up. "Who are you?"

Aamer fumbled for his cell phone but the young man kicked it to the floor. "Not a great time to make a phone call."

Shana gazed at the tall young man standing before her, then turned to her husband. "Remember I told you I was raped at a college fraternity party?"

"News like that is kind of hard to forget," David said.

"What?" came a high-pitched scream from just inside the doorway.

Shana's heart pounded like a pestle as Becca rushed to her bedside.

Her daughter enfolded her in her arms. "Is it true?"

Shana trembled as she laid her head against her daughter's breast. "Don't hate me."

"You *should* hate her," said the young man with the gun. "Your whole life has been a lie."

Her daughter turned to the young man with the gun. "Who are you? What are you doing in my mother's hospital room?"

The young man bowed low, the gun barrel following his movement. "I am your mother's kidnapper."

Becca's eyes followed the movement. "The detective said my mother's kidnapper wore alligator high-tops."

He raised one foot. "Yep, that's me."

"Asshole!" David raised his cane at him.

The young man knocked it from his hand with his gun. "Watch your language, old man."

Shana sensed her son's encroaching mood change. She sent her husband a stern glance, then pinched Becca on her arm to warn her off further dialogue. Her daughter sloughed off her hand. "Why did you kidnap my mother and take her hostage?"

Before her son could open his mouth to speak, Shana interceded. "He planned to avenge my rape."

"That makes no sense. You don't even know her!"

The young man wiggled the gun at Shana. "You wanna tell her, or should I?"

Shana raised her arms. "Don't!"

"Don't kill you or don't tell Becca who I am?"

Becca's eyes widened. "I know who you are. You're the one who's been skulking through my sister's Facebook posts. That's how you knew about our family trip to New York, about the time and location of our family brunch."

Shana's heart dropped as Daniel retrained his gun on her daughter. "Enough, Becca!"

But her daughter was stubborn. She wouldn't back down; it was in her DNA. "You expect my father and I to believe you booked a flight from Chicago to avenge the rape of a woman you've never met?"

Earlier, Shana had phoned the detective to share her theory about her captor's real name and profession. She should be there any minute. God-willing, they'd still be alive by the time she showed up.

"While we're at it, is your name really Rod Stewart?" Becca persisted.

She aches for truth over safety, like me, Shana silently lamented.

A tall, lean, bespectacled man calmly entered the room. "Rod Stewart was my favorite singer. Our family used to listen to his songs."

The young man's eyebrows rose in surprise. "Dad! What are you doing here?"

The puzzle pieces were beginning to fall in place, thought Shana.

"You said you were going to find your foster parents and ask them why they abused you, but I knew who you were really going to see. Give me the gun, son."

Rod pointed the gun at the floor instead.

"When I first saw your police sketch on the news," said Alan, "I told myself you had a double and went about my business. But I had a bad feeling in my gut, so I called your workplace and asked to speak to you."

"You only phoned me at DCFS once, when mom died."

Alan picked at his face. "That's a story we need to revisit over a beer sometime."

"You don't drink beer!"

"You told them you were taking a two-week vacation. I let myself into your apartment and checked your desk. Your laptop was gone, but I did find a rental receipt for an Air B&B that was For Sale, along with a map of Central Park."

"So you didn't kill your grandmother," guessed Shana. "The owner rented you her house until the new owners took possession!"

"I've been known to substitute fiction for truth," the young man apologized. "It's unlikely the police would suspect an empty house with a *For Sale* sign to be anything other than that. I tracked that house on *Google Satellite* after Rachel posted that your—our—family was visiting New York City and lunching at the Boat House restaurant."

"Our? What do you mean 'our'?" asked Becca.

Shana squeezed her eyes, waiting for the worst.

Instead Alan spoke. "I gotta hand it to you, son, the house was in a perfect location, twelve minutes north of park grounds."

"I know, right? I only planned to talk to my birth mother, not kill her. But she thinks I'm a bad guy."

"You are a bad guy," Shana shouted. "You kidnapped me from the park, you shackled me to a radiator, you starved me, forced me to sit in my own shit."

"Language!" Alan and the young man said simultaneously.

Becca's voice rang throughout the room. "OMG! My mom is your birth mother!"

"Darling, this all occurred decades ago," Shana called after her daughter, but she'd already buried her head in her father's shoulder.

Shana glanced at David. The hurt expression on his face made her feel sick to her stomach. Had she been shielding her husband from the truth all these years for his benefit, or had she been afraid of the repercussions her truth might bring, she wondered.

"Don't say another word, son, until I get you a lawyer," said Alan.

What a mess she had made of their lives, keeping all these truths locked in her memory. Now it was all out, and, damn it, she was glad. "You threatened to cut me up into beef soup chunks."

Rod once again aimed the gun at Shana. "She's an evil one, this mother of ours. I wanted to make her pay for giving me up at birth, for the fucked-up life that followed." He banged his forehead with the gun. "Language."

"I gave you to a loving couple who longed for a baby. You told me yourself that your first adoptive father only turned you in to DCFS because your adoptive mom died of cancer."

"Yeah? What about the foster care that followed? What about being shackled to the living room radiator while they went out to shovel the snow? Do you have any idea how hot a radiator gets when you're sitting inches away?"

Shana caught her breath. Poor—the letters of her son's real first name played roulette in her brain. She castigated herself for her thoughts still being jumbled.

"What was even more fun was being locked in a closet for sucking my thumb–I was a traumatized four-year-old forced to sit in my own bodily waste while they collected a monthly check."

But for the closet, her son had revisited his own horrors on her, thought Shana.

Alan stepped between her and their son. "Put down the gun, son," he said, his voice firm. "Your birth mother and I both know you didn't mean to hurt her; things just got out of hand."

"Out of hand?" Shana snarled.

"Does she know?" Alan asked his son.

The young man glanced at her. "If she does, I didn't tell her."

"Tell me what?" she demanded.

"This big guy is bi-polar," said Alan.

The memory hit her like a bowling ball. "I know, he told me."

"He also has anxiety disorder from his foster home abuse. That anxiety turned into full-blown panic attacks as a teenager when he was a counselor at wilderness camp, but meds helped reduce his symptoms."

Now she remembered. "He's been giving himself SSRI shots, prescription drugs he acquired illegally," she said. "And as a camp counselor, he must have learned basic healing procedures, which is why he was so eager to administer aid."

Shana's husband shrugged. "His psychological disorders are no excuse for his criminal actions."

"That remains to be seen," said Alan.

Becca inched toward her brother. "I'm sorry you had to experience this abuse, but our mom couldn't have foreseen that would happen. She did the best she could."

Shana watched as if in slow motion her son turn the gun on her daughter. "But you and your family sure didn't."

Becca retreated a step. "What are you saying?"

"You guys didn't even attempt to rescue Mom. I was prepared to die in a shoot-out, but no police came pounding on the door of the house. No hostage negotiation took place. You and your family failed the test."

Hoping to block her son from her daughter, Shana moved almost imperceptibly between them. "It doesn't matter who did what when, son. Put the gun down and let's start anew."

He'd noticed her movement and retrained the gun on her. "You want to save Becca and hang me out to dry."

David spoke up, his voice tense. "The only one who's hanging you out to dry is you, with your self-pitying attitude; an attitude you share with your mother."

"Don't bait him," Shana whispered.

"You're my wife, not my mother. It's time you start acting that way."

He was standing up to her, in front of a mad man, to boot, thought Shana.

"You don't even know me, know what I'm capable of, old man."

"You don't know me, either," said David. "If you did, you'd know the girls and I were working with the police 24/7 to rescue my wife. Her picture, along with one of you with your face hidden by an umbrella, was plastered all over the news channels, as well as social media."

"But you were too clever," interjected Aamer.

Rod turned the gun on him. "Shut up!"

"You'd also know that if I have anything to do with it, we're all walking out of here alive, including you and Aamer," said David.

"If anybody walks out of here alive, that's my decision. I know that won't include me."

Slow and steady, Shana told herself. "It doesn't have to end this way, son. Put the gun down. I promise I won't let anyone hurt you."

He smirked. "It's a little late to switch gears now, don't you think?"

Shana's eyes widened. She prayed the detective would be here any minute. Armed.

"Why are you pointing a gun at our mother if you don't want to hurt her?" Becca blurted.

He focused the gun on Becca. "Mommy could have aborted me, but she let me live. I owe her that. But she still needs to pay for abandoning me. She showered her love on you and your sister; love that was rightfully mine. It's only fair you or Rachel should die in her stead."

"Rod, don't do anything crazy," Shana pleaded.

"Why are you acting clueless? You knew my real name two days ago."

Suddenly the last missing marble, her son's real name, parachuted into Shana's brain. "Daniel!"

The young man's demeanor turned sunny at the revelation. "Wow! I was beginning to feel like Rumplestiltskin!"

"Who's Daniel?"

They all turned to find Zander about to wheel Rachel across the threshold.

"He's our brother," said Becca.

Daniel pointed his gun at them. "Nice to finally meet you."

Rachel took one look at the gun and screamed Zander whisked Rachel back out into the hallway.

Shana made a move to follow, but Daniel waved the gun in her face. "This could have been my family if you hadn't abandoned me."

David hobbled to his feet. "Don't shoot my wife. Take me instead!"

Daniel guffawed. "You'd sacrifice your life for hers, knowing she didn't trust you enough to share her truth?"

Shana's teeth chattered, but she spoke through her fear. "David, I didn't tell you about my rape and pregnancy because I didn't want to burden our new relationship with my baggage."

"Sometimes it is the best way," said Aamer.

Daniel pushed him to the floor. "Nobody asked your opinion."

Aamer rubbed his lower back. "Sorry I interrupt."

"My wife's life is what's important to me," said David. "I don't care two bits about her past!"

If only that were true, thought Shana.

Her son trained his gun on her husband. "So I'm just a mistake to delete, old man?"

"Dad didn't say you're a mistake," Becca said boldly.

"He's right." Daniel pivoted toward Shana. "You're the mistake."

Shana froze.

Alan inched his way toward Daniel. "You want to take revenge on your birth mother for subjecting you to foster care abuse, but it's not her fault; it's nobody's fault."

Daniel brandished the gun high over Alan's head, still trained on Shana. "That's what you flew here from Chicago to tell me, Dad?"

"I flew here to save your life, Daniel. I've watched three of my children die; I will not allow you to be Number Four."

Daniel's body trembled. "So Mom wasn't hallucinating when she talked about dead babies."

Shana watched Alan extend his hand toward the gun. "Mom wanted to tell you when you were in middle school. But your behavior was so unpredictable in those years, I worried you'd go off the deep end. I convinced her to wait until you were older and could handle the news…"

Daniel yanked the gun from his father's reach. "…but that day never came, did it?"

Alan looked as forlorn as she felt, thought Shana.

"Mom was never okay with you not knowing the truth. I made a mistake, forgive me."

"Did you kill my siblings, liked you killed Mom?"

Alan looked like he'd been punched in the gut. "Two of your brothers died in utero. Justin was the third baby. His first day on earth, Justin's organs had already begun to shut down. He suffered for eight days. The doctor said it would be a couple of hours or days, at most. Your mom and I couldn't bear to see him suffer. I pulled his breathing tube and let him die in peace."

Daniel pounded his forehead with the gun. "And here I thought I was an only child."

"You were an only child, at least to us, Daniel," said Alan.

"An only child reared in lies and deceit, ignorant that I had two sisters and three brothers."

Becca spoke up. "It's not all about you. Our mother blindsided me and Rachel, too."

Shana called out to Becca. "Darling, it happened so many years ago. I wanted to spare you and your sister from knowing you had a brother conceived during rape."

Daniel raised the gun to his right temple. "I am my birth mother's garbage. My foster care parents' monthly paycheck. My two adoptive families' hope. A commodity. That's all I am. That's all I've ever been."

Shana couldn't let Daniel kill another human being. She certainly couldn't allow him to kill himself. She opened her mouth to speak, but Becca beat her to it. "Go ahead, Dude. If you're going to kill yourself, get it over with."

"What are you doing?" David hissed at their daughter.

Becca paid him no heed. "Woe with you, woe with you."

Daniel glanced at her out the corner of his eye.

"All these people are vying over your love, your forgiveness. Offering you the family you were denied. But you're so wrapped up in the injustices done you, you can't see the light."

Shana held her hand to her heart; her daughter was braver than all of them put together. "Daniel, if you kill any of us, you go to prison for the rest of your life. Kill yourself, you pull the shade on all possibilities for a new future."

"Even if you're right, it makes no difference. I'll go to prison for killing your rapist."

A new voice echoed through the room. "Put your gun down on the floor and kick it across the room."

They all turned to see a plain clothes detective raise her badge with one hand as she trained her gun on Daniel with the other.

Daniel smirked at the detective as he kicked the gun across the floor. "Sure, no problem."

Her eyes still trained on Daniel, Detective Hernandez bent for the gun. The very same instant Daniel rammed his body into hers, throwing her off balance.

Aamer pulled a pocketknife and was approaching from behind.

Shana placed herself between Aamer and her son. "No!"

Daniel turned to see her arms raised to protect him. Tears fell from his cheeks.

Becca grabbed the gun from the floor and pointed it at her brother.

He pivoted to look at her, a tiny smile on his lips. "Are you your brother's keeper?"

Aamer placed the knife at Daniel's ribs. "Do not move!"

Daniel back-slapped the knife away, just as Alan began pounding the burly man with his fists. "My son's already put down his gun. Leave him alone."

Taking advantage of the moment, David threw a Styrofoam glass of water at Daniel's feet, and he slid onto his backside.

"Enough!" shouted Shana. "I refuse to have anybody's blood on my conscience!"

Detective Hernandez pushed through the family, leaned down, and cuffed Daniel's hands. "You are under arrest for assaulting a police officer, and for holding a gun on innocent bystanders."

"What about for killing his birth father?" shouted Shana.

"Lucky for him, Daniel does not excel at slicing body parts."

"Body parts?" cried Alan.

"His birth father is recuperating from shoulder surgery at a hospital less than an hour from here."

"He refused to admit I was his son," cried Daniel.

Detective Hernandez mumbled into her radio. "Tell the police to stand down. Hostage under control."

"Un-cuff my son and let me take him home," said Alan.

"No fuckin' way, and don't you dare say 'language'!" shouted Shana. "We've been doing everything possible to save Daniel's life. Reality is, my son kidnapped me and left me in the woods to die!"

"But you didn't die, did you?" Alan said calmly. "And you've only sustained a minor cut on your cheek, so…."

Detective Hernandez blocked the doorway. "Nobody's going anywhere."

David hobbled towards Daniel. "You promised not to harm my wife."

"Harm her? I wanted to save her, just like my dad saved my mom."

"What are you talking about?" asked David.

"Dementia caused my mom to lose her mind and bodily functions. She was even forgetting how to swallow. She was fading fast. My dad wanted me to be free of her. To live my life. But he didn't want to wait for God to finish the job, so he removed her breathing tube, just like he did my brother."

A collective gasp filled the room.

Alan's face paled. "How did you…?"

"You did what you had to do to free mom and me both."

Alan buried his head in his arms.

"When mom was still able to talk, she called me 'Justin.' She kept apologizing for letting you remove my breathing tube—Justin's breathing tube."

Alan sighed. "Your mom and the doctor agreed that I remove your brother's breathing tube; his organs were slowly shutting down and we wanted to spare him hours of needless suffering before his encroaching death. Even the rabbi agreed it was the compassionate thing to do. But deep within, I tormented myself with the possibility that unhooking that tube freed me and Mom from being consigned to a living hell should Justin have miraculously survived."

Shana shivered upon hearing his confession. But who was she to judge? Hadn't she also done what she did for her baby's greater good?

"I performed that same last compassionate step for your mother, as well."

Detective Hernandez stepped in front of Alan. "Hold out your wrists, sir."

Alan's jaw dropped. "Wh-a-t?"

The detective snapped the handcuffs. "Illinois' euthanasia laws do not permit mercy killings. They only allow signed, dated, and witnessed Do Not Resuscitate directives."

"But my wife did agree to removing all death delaying procedures," Alan protested.

"Did she put it in writing?"

"No, but we discussed it as she went downhill."

"No paper trail, you're SOL," said the detective.

"What mean this SOL?" interrupted Aamer.

"Shit out of luck," David said loudly. Everybody turned to stare.

"I do speak up every now and then!"

"It's okay, Mom would understand," Daniel whispered. "Only God is perfect."

Becca looked him straight in the eye. "Did you even bother to consider that your actions may have caused our sister to go into premature labor? Do you feel guilty that at this very moment your niece's existence might be in jeopardy?"

Daniel appeared shell-shocked.

"But taking revenge on my mom for abandoning you was more important."

Daniel covered his eyes. "I don't know."

They all watched Detective Hernandez read both Daniel and Alan their Miranda rights and escort them to two police officers waiting in the hall.

Becca rushed from the room. Shana suspected she was going to check on Rachel. She began to inch herself out of bed, prepared to go after her, when the detective reentered the room. "Daniel and Alan Stewart will be held in custody overnight. Considering the seriousness of these offenses, the judge probably will hold them without bond."

Shana directed her gaze to the detective. "Will I be forced to testify against my son?"

"I'd discuss that with an attorney, if I were you," said the detective. "The DA will probably have enough evidence to prosecute, either way." The detective strode out of the room.

"Are you nuts?" David asked, his voice incredulous. "Daniel admitted to stabbing his birth father. He attacked a police officer. He held all of us hostage. And you don't want to testify against him in a court of law?"

Shana put her hand on his cheek. "Right now, I need to check on my daughter and grandbaby."

Aamar stepped forward. "It is time for me to bid you salaam. Peace. May we meet again in better times."

Ugh! Discussing all this private stuff in front of Aamer was not smart. He'd tell Oma, then she'd tell Zander, then he'd tell Rachel, then....

David stopped her ruminations. "You cannot let Daniel go free," said David.

Shana eyed her husband with a new respect. Her sleeping bear, awakened from a forty-year hibernation. If only he understood her reticence. "He is my son, David. Wouldn't you move heaven and earth if, God forbid, it was Rachel or Becca?"

"Rachel and Becca wouldn't be stupid enough to pull shit like that."

"Language," she snickered. "Feeling lost and abandoned makes people do weird things."

"There's no way you can excuse his actions!"

"Nobody's talking 'excuse.' But is jail the right place for him?"

"That's up to a judge and jury to determine, not you. Right now, we have a daughter and grandbaby to worry about."

Sighing, Shana pressed the nurse's button.

The nurse hurried into the room. "What do you need?"

"Please bring me a wheelchair. I need to get to the maternity ward."

"Will do."

Shana and David watched her exit the room.

"You coming along?"

"We need to talk."

For the first time in years, her husband was making a proactive communication overture about something *deep*. Brave new world. "Afterward. I promise."

Shana wondered whether their *talk* would produce positive or negative consequences for their relationship. Their marriage was definitely worth fighting for.

Chapter 65

SHANA

Shana's eyes sparkled as she peered through the glass incubator. Weighing in at 2.5 pounds, Kensington lay attached to a vast assortment of needle-sized tubes and monitors, as well as a breathing apparatus. But as far as she was concerned, her grandbaby was perfect. "She's beautiful!"

Her oldest daughter squeezed her hand. Then she reached through a tiny opening in the incubator to touch her infant's fingers. "I can't believe she really came out of me," she cooed.

Shana watched Zander reach through another hole to touch the baby's feet. He and Rachel would be loving parents, this she knew without doubt.

Becca made kissing sounds through a third opening.

"Honey, you probably don't want to breathe into the baby's sterile space," Shana suggested hesitantly. Now that her most recent escapade was over, she didn't want to cause any tension with her daughters by offering unsolicited advice.

"Mom's right," Rachel said softly. "We all sanitized our hands and phones before entering the Neonatal Unit."

"So now we need to sanitize our breath?" Becca joked.

"Don't breathe into the incubator and you don't have to worry," Shana said lightly. Worriedly, she glanced at her daughters; they were too enamored with the baby to acknowledge her comment.

"She is the teensiest, tiniest, most gorgeous thing," her son-in-law marveled.

"The doctor says she's a real fighter," boasted Rachel.

David hugged their son-in-law. "She comes from strong stock."

Oma, Zander's mom, entered the hospital room, depositing an edible fruit basket on the sink counter. "How is our baby today?"

Shana gave her a welcoming smile. "Doctor says her condition is stable, thank God."

Zan maneuvered around the incubator, taking pics of the baby from his phone. "She's gotta stay in the hospital for six to ten weeks, until her lungs develop and she can breathe on her own."

"They're making sure Kensington doesn't have any brain bleeds, and that all her organs are functioning okay," said Rachel. "Ooh, I can't wait to be able to pick her up."

"I thought you're nursing, Rach," said Becca.

"Her milk hasn't come in yet," said Zan. "Volunteers are expressing milk. Then that milk goes through a tiny tube and into the baby's nostrils."

David looked impressed. "You sure know a lot about nursing."

"That's 'cause he breastfeeds," teased Rachel.

Zan grinned at her daughter. "You wish."

"Your fruit basket looks yummy!" said Becca.

"All mamas know food is at the heart of every celebration," said Oma.

Shana bit into a chocolate covered pineapple lollipop. "It's crazy that Kenzie's already been on this earth for two days."

Zan playfully poked Rachel in the shoulder. "Told you everybody's going to call her Kenzie."

Rachel poked him back. "That's not happening."

Becca giggled. "You are such a control freak."

Which was just what Shana had been thinking.

"My baby, my rules."

"I wasn't in on making that rule," said Zan.

"Your rules don't count," Rachel said, her tone snarky.

Shana and David exchanged glances. *See? It's not always my fault*, she wanted to tell him. Instead she kept mum, thankful that this family gathering had not been convened for a different purpose. Gazing at her whole family gathered together in this room of new beginnings, she experienced a feeling of pure bliss.

A voice boomed from the hallway. Aamer crossed the threshold. "Praise Allah, today has come."

If Shana had entered the room before thoroughly washing her hands, she'd be dead meat. But she kept her mouth shut and let the dice fall where they may.

Oma intercepted her husband as he stepped inside. "Did you scrub your hands for five minutes?"

"I need no washing of hands. I bring gift for baby, then I go."

Oma groaned. "You must wash your hands before you come in so the baby does not catch your germs." She steered him back into the hallway.

David hobbled over to where Shana stood munching a chocolate covered cherry. "You all right?" he whispered. "You haven't said more than a couple of words to Rachel today."

"I'm getting there," she promised.

Her husband turned to the rest of the family. "We're going to the snack machine. Anybody want anything?"

No thanks echoed through the room. David ushered her out of the room and into the hallway. "Getting where? You can't still be obsessing about the argument you and the girls had at the restaurant!"

"Maybe I am, maybe I'm not," Shana pouted.

"You know I love you."

"Really, 'cause you haven't told me for a long time."

"Yeah, well you were off getting kidnapped and tortured, so…."

Shana giggled at his gallows humor. "True, I have been incognito for a few days."

David's voice turned serious. "What were you thinking, storming out of the restaurant and into unfamiliar surroundings without a phone or money?"

Shana shrugged. "I felt abandoned. I didn't care what happened to me. I didn't think you guys cared, either."

"There you go, playing the victim card again. *Nobody appreciates me.* It's not always all about you."

"You're right," she admitted.

Her husband looked taken aback. "I am?"

"I have been acting like a victim since the kids were young. They had no problem opening their mouths at me, but for you, they were perfect."

"I wouldn't say *perfect*," David countered.

"Over the years, you continually sided with them over me in every argument."

"You're exaggerating," he protested.

"Perception is reality, like shooting your photos from different angles, right?"

He began to respond but she shushed him with one finger—not the middle one. "I'm a retired journalist, a wife, the mother of two grown kids, a first-time grandparent. No longer can I lazily allow words to fall from my tongue because I know you guys can't fire me.

"I need to stop giving advice unless asked for, and to choose more carefully the questions I ask and the comments I make, thinking first how those personal questions and comments may strike others in our family."

David eyes widened. "Can I get this down in writing?"

"That said, I no longer will be at everybody's beck and call. You guys have proved you can stand on your collective feet quite well without my butting in."

"Wait while I get the kids. They need to hear this."

"Shut up and let me finish."

"You doing the Gettysburg address, or what?" he joked.

She gave him the death stare.

David raised his hands in surrender.

"Lastly, I will be visiting my son in jail—in prison, if it comes to that. I don't want to hear any backlash from you, got it?"

David's posture stiffened.

"You don't want me to build a relationship with my son?"

"I didn't say that."

"But that's what you were thinking."

"Whatever," his voice dejected.

"Don't cave, talk to me," she pleaded.

"As usual, you claim to know my thoughts," he said bitterly.

Her husband's arrow had struck its target within her heart. "I'll try to stop inserting my words into your mouth," she said.

"Don't *try*, just do it!"

What was it about love that made you hurt the one you're with, she wondered. "I apologize for being hurtful. I definitely need to work on my personal shtick."

He turned back to her. "That you do, because I'm not going to be your batting ball anymore."

"Respect goes both ways. I need you to stand up for me when the kids put me down."

"You bring a lot of their retaliation on yourself."

"That's part of the shtick I'm working on. Still, I need to feel confident that you're on my side. Hell, I was almost killed two days ago…"

"…at the hands of your son," interrupted David.

"Yes, at the hands of my son," Shana lamented. "I deserve to be buoyed up, here."

"I'm sorry you don't feel supported by me."

It was true that he did emotionally support her in the majority of her endeavors, but when it came to their daughters, all bets were off. Still, the last thing Shana wanted to deal with was the familiar *woe with me* in her husband's voice. She changed subject. "By the way, I've decided to volunteer as a social activist."

David's jaw dropped. "What?"

"All my newspaper years, I've watched politicians make self-serving decisions that affect our collective freedom. I've got the knowledge, and I've got the time, to work with organizations I believe in."

"Too many new decisions for me to absorb in one day. How's that even going to happen with you flying back and forth to New York to see Rachel and the baby, as well as visiting your son in jail? And what about me? I don't want to be alone."

"Come with me, then!"

"It's hard enough for me to get around as it is. Who knows how long it'll be before I end up in a wheelchair."

"Now who's playing *victim*? Your doctor said you're in good health. You'll be fine."

"Do you still love me?" he asked solemnly.

Shana pulled him to her and kissed him passionately. "More than ever."

He broke from her embrace. "There's one more thing you need to promise me."

"I thought you wanted to eat."

"No more lies."

"I don't lie all that much," Shana protested.

David spelled it. "No lies of addition, no lies of omission." She'd try. She'd really try. "I promise."

"It still hurts that you kept thirty years of secrets from me."

"I get it."

"We've got to be able to trust each other with the truth."

"Agreed."

"Even if you know the kids and I will be mad at you for something you do, you've got to come clean. Better yet, think before doing something that you know will send us reeling."

"Enough, already. Let's go eat."

David stared her in the eyes. "Otherwise, I'm leaving. I mean that with all sincerity."

Shana felt her husband's resolve. "In return, I need you to not blow up at me when I do mess up. Neither of us are perfect. I also need you to share your feelings with me, not just trivial day-to-day stuff, either."

It was David's turn to sigh. "I'll do my best. Don't expect miracles."

Although unsure if they both could live up to their renewed commitment to one another, Shana thrilled at the possibility. "Our marriage contract says for better or worse, in sickness and health. In good times and bad times.

I do.

Love you.

Forever."

Book Discussion Questions

1. What was your first impression of Shana Kahn? Why?
2. How did you react to Shana's interaction with Zander's stepfather? Why?
3. Why did Rachel and Becca feel that their mother had embarrassed them?
4. If you were Shana, would you have reacted in a similar or different manner during the brunch argument? Why?
5. How did you feel toward Rachel and Becca? Did your view of them change?
6. What were your first/later impressions of David as a husband and father?
7. How did Daniel's backstory, told through the eyes of this adoptive parents, enhance the plot?
8. How did you feel about Daniel in the beginning? How did your view of him change, if at all, by the end?
9. How did Shana and her daughters change, if any, throughout the book?
10. Were you surprised at the end? Why or why not?

RESOURCES

*Rules of Estrangement;
Why Adult Children Cut Ties &
How to Heal the Conflict*
by Joshua Coleman, PhD

*Raising Adopted Children:
A Manual for Adoptive Parents
by Lois Ruskai Melina*

*The Open Adoption Experience
A Complete Guide for Adoptive
and Birth Families
by Lois Ruskai Melina
and Sharon Kaplan Roszia*

Psychobabble

CHAPTER 1

Boom! Boom! I attempt to nestle my head one iota deeper into the sponge-sheathed frames, but the cacophony within the MRI machine slams my brain like a hurricane.

Desperate, I mouth a mantra: Breathe in. Breathe out.

My mantra gives me the finger.

Silence. A flicker of hope. Then the shattering assault resumes. A stray tear slides down my cheek, but my arms are shackled.

A muffled voice floats into the steel cavern. "Sixty seconds, Dr. Cook. Don't move."

As if! Encased within this machine, my body is helpless. My imagination, however, is free to seek its own music pedagogy as it frenetically attempts to adapt to this orchestra of the inferno. In my mind, I raise my arms to navigate a fragmented soprano line high above the vigorous sound waves. I lower my arms to direct the pounding bass section. I'm just beginning to flow into this peculiar rhythm when the AB/AB sequence ends abruptly. I start to hyperventilate.

"You're doing fine," the technician mumbles through the loudspeaker. "Five minutes 'til your injection."

Mentally, I twist a pillow case. Why didn't I reschedule my MRI until someone could accompany me? At the very least, I should have registered Tiffany, my rescue cat, as a service animal, because—dirty little secret—there's nobody I could have asked. Well, almost nobody. I could have asked the other psychologist at Jessica Reed Center, but the new Mrs. Yuliya Gulabchikava is enjoying her honeymoon in Spain this weekend.

Then there's Juanita, our office receptionist. In my two years at the domestic violence Center, I've become friendly with the young single mom, stopping for a quick chat as I tie my Nikes and head out for a lunchtime jog. She even cat-sits for me. But with her full-time job and four kids under age ten, she's too busy to take a pee, let alone accompany me to the doctor.

I could have tracked Glenn on Facebook, but that would be awkward. I haven't spoken to my ex-husband in eight years.

The muffled voice booms. "Raise your foot if you need something."

If I need something? After undergoing three months of every diagnostic test imaginable for memory loss and erratic behavior, what I need is for this horror movie to be over! So far, all my physical and cognitive tests have come back negative. That's only because I haven't hit the right test yet. Today's MRI will determine if I have Alzheimer's or a Brain Aneurysm. I start to tremble, thinking about what wither diagnosis would mean.

"Coming to check on you now," the voice blasts over the loudspeaker.

The incessant banging ceases. A welcome silence saturates every nook and cranny of the sterile room. A plumpish, dark-skinned technician approaches. She releases the steel casing above my face and upper body. Then she gently inserts a needle into the catheter taped to the top of my hand. "I'm injecting dye into your veins for a contrasting image."

I shiver at the sight of the menacing needle, even though I know it won't be touching my skin. "My clients should see me now."

"You work around here?"

"JRDVC."

The technician withdraws the needle. "The domestic violence center?"

I nod.

"My brother, Gilbert, he got sent there. He doin' fifty hours community service 'cause he beat up Tahisha so bad."

"Did your brother get Judge Collingsworth, by any chance?"

"You know him?"

"Julian Collingsworth is the most lenient of the six Cook County judges who hear domestic violence cases. So who's Tahisha?"

"She his girlfriend. Got herself pregnant by another man. That's how come my brother hauled off and hit her."

"Sounds like your brother's got anger management issues."

"Gilbert, he always had a mean old temper. Takes after my momma. She a tornado with a belt when we was growin' up." The med tech closes the contraption and exits the room, calling back to me, "Two minutes."

Back inside the gladiator mask, the hammering resumes, but my attention is now otherwise occupied. I parachute into a fantasy designed to punish the technician's brother. Whip in hand, I handcuff Gilbert to a dozen domestic violence victims who scream out their heartache. Finally I paint a red "L" for Loser on his forehead, strip him naked, and video tape him delivering a high school presentation on domestic abuse from the perspective of the abuser. My punishment is as fair as any judge could mete out.

In my fantasy, I'm as naked as Gilbert!

Wow! I really am hard up. Can't even remember the last time I encouraged a hook-up; one more casualty of divorce.

The med tech is at my side once again, releasing my head from its steel bondage. "There, now. That wasn't so bad, was it?"

Compared to being hit by a tsunami, it's a breeze. I attempt to sit up and promptly fall back on the steel table.

She places an ice pack beneath my neck. "You not the only one who gets dizzy after being harnessed to this here machine for forty-five minutes."

Surrendering to the moment, I lie still, ice pack in place. "It helped when I heard your voice, even though it came through muffled."

"Yeah, well this baby be malfunctioning this morning. We tried calling you to reschedule, but nobody answered."

Darn. I could have saved myself the trip. "I forget my cell phone these days."

"Not too good for your patients, huh?"

This time, I sit up and swing my legs over the side of the table. "I'm not so indispensable. Most of my clients see a psychiatrist one-on-one."

I can't prescribe meds, so no ties. Just the way I like it.

"Feeling dizzy?"

"My neck's a bit stiff."

"That's normal. In a couple a' days we'll be sending copies of your MRI results to your neurologist and your referring doctor. Hey, I got to be bringing up the next patient. You had us running a half-hour late, you know."

"Sorry. My alarm clock never went off." More likely, I forgot to set it.

The technician grins. "All right, then. Snow's supposed to turn to ice this afternoon. Take care you don't slip out there. Crazy weather this early in December."

I chuckle. "You're obviously not from Chicago."

The tech takes my elbow and steers me down the hall. "Moved here from Atlanta in 2015. Knew I'd have to be worrying about snow, not about no serial killer."

"Don't believe everything you read," I say.

"That story's been playin' on the TV, 24/7. The dude's already killed four people."

"Listen, it's been three weeks. If we really had a serial killer in our midst, the CPD would have caught him by now."

"Maybe he be smarter than the police."

"In the 1960s, we had a serial killer who systematically tortured, raped, and murdered eight student nurses. He was arrested pronto when a hospital doctor recognized his tattoo."

"The police didn't find him, the doctor did," said the tech.

"We're talking fifty-one years ago. Long before modern technology."

She dropped me off at the locker room entrance. "I'm still gonna be watching my back."

Without thinking, I blurt: "By the way, did your brother's girlfriend lose her baby?"

The MRI tech's eyes widened. "You sure ain't never gonna be my therapist!"

Without another word, she stomps out of the locker room.

Horrified, I run to the doorway and shout down the hall. "I am so sorry!"

My words echo into the empty corridor.

I can't believe I asked her that. Lately, weird utterances have been spewing from my lips. Tourette's Syndrome, I wonder. What is wrong with me?

In my deep despair, a vintage TV commercial jingle reverberates through my head.

Only your hairdresser knows for sure.